Running with Motorcycles

Marcia Kelbon

Running with Motorcycles
First edition, published 2022

By Marcia Kelbon

Cover Illustration by Barbara Ford

Copyright © 2022, Marcia Kelbon

ISBN-13: 978-1-952685-47-7

Published by Kitsap Publishing
P.O. Box 572
Poulsbo, WA 98370
www.KitsapPublishing.com

Dedication

To Richard, who has always supported my dreams, including living in the woods, riding motorcycles, and sharing our lives with a series of much-loved dogs.

Chapter 1

Later

Will and Hunter scrambled as fast as they could up the slope from the forested ravine, and then darted into the loamy hollow under a gnarled old fir log. They hunkered low under the overhanging grey-green moss and tried not to think about how many beetles might be crawling around in the rubble of the damp punk wood that lined the hole in which they sheltered. "Shhh, Hunter," whispered Will, drawing his dog in close. Hunter reacted to the stress emanating from Will, understanding on an instinctive level that there was some threat approaching. The dog nuzzled his soft nose and velvety whiskers into the crook of Will's neck, and Will stroked his damp mottled brown fur. Each calmed the other as their breathing slowed and, finally, Will thought they were safe.

But then the still air was disturbed by the crack of a branch breaking just a short distance away on the opposite hill. Will and Hunter pressed down still further into the damp earth, trying not to make a sound. Will thought feverishly of how he could defend Hunter if they were found. The rustle of leaves and crackling of fallen branches told him the tracker was drawing close.

Chapter 2

Now

Another blackberry vine had been sucked into the cog on his axle, stopping his chain as surely as a trap on a coyote's paw. Will needed to get home but hopped off his bike to clear out the bits of leaves and fiber. He could not help but notice how the setting sun bathed the rocks and tree stumps with an ember glow, set off against the electric green of the myriad fir, hemlock and cedar trees, bracken and sword ferns, and numerous berry bushes. As the last of the warm summer light was disappearing behind the foothills, he knew there would be heck to pay if he did not make it down to his family's cabin before it was gone completely. Will gave his bike a running start down the hill as he jumped on when out of the corner of his eye he saw a brown and tan streak duck behind the salal brush. He braked hard – what was that? It was too small for a bear cub, and it moved wrong for a coyote. Could that be a marten? Will would love to find out but rather than spend the next week confined to the house, he made haste for home before all that was left was twilight.

"Pass me the potato salad, would you Will," said Will's father, Dan. "Pruning all those Christmas trees makes me as hungry as a spring bear and your mom sure is a good cook." Will had to agree as he helped himself to more pieces of barbecue chicken. His mother Emma just smiled, because nothing felt better than seeing her family eat well. She knew how much energy her husband burned through in their tree farm and her rambunctious son used exploring the surrounding foothills of the Olympic peninsula. "I might have seen a marten by a big old fir stump as I came back from my ride today," Will said excitedly. "I heard they were coming back in the Olympics and I want to see if I can find it first thing tomorrow morning."

"Hold on a minute Will," said Emma. "You know martens are supposed to be ferocious fighters and, pound-for-pound, I would rather go up against a pit bull. The last thing we need is you getting bit by one of those overgrown weasels." Will responded hopefully, "Well it would be a lot better if I had a dog to go with me, it would keep me safe."

Emma just sighed and exchanged a knowing look with his father. "Will, we have been through this before, you know we cannot afford a GenDog right now. We would love to get you one but it is just not in the budget until a few more tree fields have grown and been harvested," said Emma. "It is not like when I was a boy," added Dan. "Why we used to have our pick of puppies from Craigslist ads, or at the shelters, or even at pet stores. We always had one or two dogs to play with and keep the farm safe. But things have changed. So, keep saving your allowance and maybe one day you will have enough to buy a cat. How does that sound?"

Will nodded and went back to picking at his chicken, the fat on which had congealed at the same rate that his appetite seemed to vanish like the morning mist. He did not want to make his folks feel bad and wanted them to believe he was happy. And mostly he was. What ten-year-old would not want to spend all summer riding his mountain bike, climbing trees, eating berries, trying to catch chipmunks, and spying on all sorts of wildlife? But no, he did not want a cat! Sure, cats were OK and all, but you could not wrestle with a cat, throw it a stick, or go exploring in the woods with a cat. It just wasn't the same.

Will thought his friend Ryan had it made. His parents gifted him with his GenDog retriever, Hank, when Ryan turned five. Hank had been genetically engineered precisely to have a life span that all but ensured Ryan would have a healthy companion until Ryan approached 80 years old. The U.S. Canine Enhancement and Rewards Tenet (CERT) Act passed in 2032 made sure of that. Ryan lived in town and did not have Will's freedom to roam the wild clear-cuts and hills. But, if he was being honest with himself, Will had to admit that he was jealous to see Hank walk Ryan to school every day and wait patiently outside for him to come out at the end of class, golden fur sprawled on the grass.

Will knew his folks did not make the kind of money that Ryan's Mom, one of the town's few lawyers, made. More than anything, Will wished he could just have an old-fashioned dog. He did not understand why GenDogs were supposed to be so much better. His Dad had explained that scientists had found a way to lengthen the telomeres, the caps found on the end of GenDog's chromosomes that grew shorter as dogs age, and that Gen-Dogs were fed restricted calorie diets, to make them age slower. And they had used a technique called CRISPR to splice in some key genes from long-lived tortoises and to remove other gene mutations associated with cancers and myopathies that caused life-shortening diseases, yielding dogs that had life spans to match humans. But Will still thought that a dog was a dog, although GenDogs were a lot more expensive than dogs used to be. As much as his father promised things would free up in the future, Will suspected he would be a grown man before there was money to spare for such a luxury.

With Will hard asleep in the cabin loft, Emma said "I sure hate to keep disappointing that boy. What was so bad about the dogs we had when we were his age? Yes, it broke my heart every time one grew old and died. But oh, it was so good to have them." "I know," said Dan. "Especially my old hound Buck. I think of him when he was young, so full of energy and slobber. He wagged his tail with his whole body! That dog was my best friend from the time I was eight to just a year after I met you at WSU.”

And I remember how depressed you were when you finally had to put him down that one Thanksgiving visit back home,” responded Emma. “I did not think you would ever be yourself again.”

“I still just wish I had been given the chance to go into the vet’s back room with him,” said Dan. “I will always recall that look he gave me over his shoulder as he was led away.” Dan remembered how Buck’s muzzle was heavily flecked with grey, and how he had hobbled painfully along with two bad hips. But his brown eyes, though cloudy, still held a deep love for Dan and unquestioning trust as he took a last look at Dan. Dan’s eyes misted up all these years later. Gathering himself after a moment, he cleared his throat and sighed. “Maybe it is better, after all, not to have that heartache with a GenDog.”

Chapter 3

In the morning Will bolted down his eggs, bacon, and toast, sliding a crust of bread inside his shorts pocket before anyone noticed. As he rushed to clear his plate and head outside, Emma said "Hold on their cowboy, aren't you forgetting something? You know those chickens won't feed themselves." He should have known better than to think his mother would ever let him forget his chores, Will thought, as he grabbed a basket and scoop of scratch. Out to the coop he went, opening the door to see small dust motes floating in the sunshine as he was hit with the pungent aroma of layered straw and chicken manure. He hastily pushed under each warm, soft hen setting in a nest box, then made himself slow to gently remove the fresh eggs without flustering the birds too much. After feeding and watering the hens, Will passed the basket of eggs to his Mom as he ran through the cabin. Out the back door, he grabbed his old Schwinn mountain bike that was a tad too large for him but took him on many adventures.

Will strained happily as he made the climb up from his family's tree farm to the first ridge in the neighboring 320-acre replanted clear-cut. This consisted of a vast stretch of reddish-brown old-growth and second-growth stumps, canopied by deep green young Douglas fir trees that had been replanted after the last logging and had already grown to perhaps 60 feet tall. The young firs were interspersed by occasional mature trees that had been spared during the last logging and wild young trees of various species including bushy-fronded cedar, pale green big leaf maple, and dull green red alder. In addition to the stumps from logging during prior generations, the trees overlooked downed decaying logs and patches of brush and lime-green ferns. All of this nature was crisscrossed by a system of gravel logging roads and grassy skid paths.

Standing on his petals, Will soon reached the old-growth fir stump where he thought he had seen the marten the day before. The stump was a magnificent specimen, still easily ten feet across even after many decades of decay. Young wild fir and hemlock seedlings and light green huckleberry bushes, laden with bright red berries, sprouted from its top. Will found a large boulder that was baking in a patch of sun and settled down on it to wait. The morning sun was already causing the evergreens to imbue the air with a scent that was a mixture of Christmas greenery and cedar pencil shavings.

Not immediately spying anything of interest, Will arose and picked a few of the red huckleberries, enjoying the sweet pop of these between his teeth. He then wandered and studied the ground, amazed as always by how much life teemed there, that was normally unseen but came into view if one stilled and narrowed their focus. Little red fire ants climbed on to and were brushed off of his boot while larger black carpenter ants trailed back and forth to the base of the stump. He knew his father hated those big, industrious ants given the damage they could cause to a structure, drilling a small hole into a two-by-four and hollowing it out from the inside. But out here, he figured the carpenter ants were merely serving their role of slowly and painstakingly returning deadwood to the earth, and he let them be. He found a shiny black garter snake with red pinstripes down its back and had fun following it through the brush, blocking its path and making it divert its way around the toe of his boot, secure in the knowledge that there were no venomous snakes in the Olympics. Will then climbed the stump and aimed at surrounding trees and stumps with a stick held like a rifle, pretending to be an early settler hunting for supper.

Will idled away some time exploring with his imagination in this way, then returned to his perch on the sunny rock to wait again. After an hour or so his eyes started getting droopy when some movement over by the old stump caught the edge of his sight. Wide awake again, Will held his breath as he saw brown and tawny fur start creeping out of the brush. But to his surprise, it was not a marten at all – no, it was a young dog, a half-grown pup! The young canine was medium-sized, perhaps 30 pounds in weight and very lean. The pup was focused on something in the foreground as he stalked forward and did not see Will, who by good fortune had sat downwind of the stump. The dog crept onward, coming into full view. Will could see that it had what he imagined to be soft brown fur on its back and head, with a tawny mask on its face and matching tawny fur down its throat and belly. One ear flopped down like on a Labrador retriever, and one folded over halfway up, like on a bulldog or greyhound, the contrast giving the dog a somewhat comical look. Black markings perched like brows over its eyes, and a brushy tail had a white tip that matched the white tips of the dog's two front paws. Suddenly the dog pounced, nearly catching a chipmunk chewing at a fir cone that had been its intended prey. The spunky little chipmunk ran up to the top of a tree and scolded the dog so ardently that Will could not help but laugh out loud. At this sound, the pup startled, looked at Will, and bounded off and out of sight.

Will's excitement at finding a dog – a real live dog! – was muted by regret that he had scared it off. He spent some time whistling to see if the dog would come back out but had no luck. Then it dawned on him that the dog had not caught the chipmunk and was probably hungry. He must sometimes have success at hunting to be surviving out here. "Hunter – that's what I will call you!" exclaimed Will, already hatching a plan to see if he could catch and keep the pup. "Here Hunter, it's not much, but hopefully it will fill your belly," said Will as he removed the bread crust and laid it on the rock that he had been sitting on. "You had better hurry if you want to beat that chipmunk to this. I will bring you something better tomorrow." Will then grabbed his bike and rode back down for lunch and afternoon chores.

Chapter 4

"Mom, Mom, I found a dog! A puppy! In the woods. I don't think it belongs to anybody – can I keep it?" shouted Will excitedly as he burst into the kitchen. Emma, wearing worn jeans dirty from working the trees with Dan, was just finishing serving up hot grilled cheese sandwiches, golden goo oozing out from the cut centers, to go with steaming bowls of tomato soup. She paused, calmly continuing her work while considering what Will had said. "Go wash up Will, let's talk about it over lunch."

Just then Dan banged into the cabin, plopping tiredly down on a chair inside the mudroom outside of the kitchen to unlace his worn Danner boots. "Dad, I found a dog! I think it's hungry. If I catch it, can I keep it?" Will started wolfing down his sandwich, dunking each bite into soup, as he looked expectantly from his Mom to his Dad and back.

"Now Will, it's probably a GenDog that somebody owns, is missing mightily, and ought to find. And if it's not a GenDog, well, you know those are not permitted anymore," said Emma gently. She was referring to how the CERT Act, when first passed fifteen years earlier, had required all naturally occurring dogs to be spayed or neutered. People could enjoy their current dogs for the remainder of their natural lives, but, with very few exceptions, the legislature did not want natural dogs to keep breeding. This was in part intended to avoid the possibility of a GenDog and a natural dog breeding and producing pups that would have a who-knows-what sort of life span. It still seemed odd to Emma that the U.S. Congress had come together to pass the CERT Act, initiated by a pair of congressmen that were active in dog rescue circles and who each bereaved the then-recent loss of a loved dog. The CERT Act had been actively lobbied for by a strange coalition of animal rescue organizations and genetic engineering industry groups. Emma also suspected that there may have been gifts of GenDog pups to key members of the House and Senate to seal the deal. Regardless, it had been passed and signed into law by the President. The stated goals of CERT were lofty: to once and for all end the scourge of homeless and abandoned dogs having to be euthanized each year in shelters while also saving humans the pain of losing their beloved pets too early. But Emma shuddered to think about how the authorities were locating and dispatching young natural dogs now that only a few oldsters remained.

"But Mom, I don't think this is a GenDog. It has a really pretty mix of fur colors, not like any I have ever seen on a purebred GenDog", said Will. "And it is pretty skinny. I know it is hunting —I have decided to name it Hunter! But I don't think it is catching enough food."

"Will, that is enough!" exploded Dan, banging the table for emphasis. "We have been over this. I would love to buy you a GenDog pup but we just cannot afford one. And we are not going to have you bringing home some natural stray. Period! Did you know that there is a $10,000 fine for harboring a non-permitted natural dog? We just don't have that kind of money, and if we did, we would use it to plant a couple more tree fields. Now finish your lunch, we have more work to do today, and you will be helping us." Will dejectedly finished his meal, knowing that once his father took such a firm stance further argument was of no use.

That afternoon, Emma and Dan continued their work on shearing the young trees growing in rows. They each wielded sword-like machetes, whisking them quickly up and down the sides of the trees. The rapid slash of the machetes removed the end bits of the branches so that each branch of the young Christmas trees would bush out to make the tree fuller during the next growing season, while also ensuring the tree each had the desired pyramidal shape.

Not tall enough yet to do shearing, Will worked on an adjacent row of trees, pulling out weeds, particularly blackberry and Scotch broom starts, that were easy to remove while small but which would grow to choke out the trees if left unchecked. Some of the young trees were squat and very bushy, and it was clear that they had been subject to heavy deer browse the prior winter. His father teased Will good-naturedly that this is what the trees would look like if someone of Will's height did the shearing. So, it was left to Will to do the hot, sweaty weeding. Will knew that his folks needed the help and did not mind pitching in. He could not help, however, thinking the whole time he worked of the young dog up in the woods and wondering whether it had enough to eat.

Chapter 5

The following Saturday Will finally had a day to himself to do whatever he pleased. He was itchy to go check on Hunter (as he was already calling the dog in his head, despite his parents' admonishments). But first, his Dad offered to give Will a ride into town to see Ryan. Will had not had a chance to hang out with Ryan since the school was out, so he figured he best take advantage of the opportunity. Dan hoisted Will's bicycle into the back of their pickup and they rode down the three-mile gravel road to town, jostling along as they traversed ruts but enjoying the forest-cooled air that streamed through their windows.

They soon arrived at the local hardware store, which functioned as a general store selling most anything someone in the rural community could need. Will hopped out, grabbed his bike, and pedaled off to find Ryan. "Make sure you are back in time for dinner" hollered Dan. "Will do" answered Will, as he calculated how long he should visit with Ryan while still leaving time to try and find Hunter again.

Will rode by Ryan's house, a neat two-story surrounded by a well-manicured lawn, landscaped shrubs, and impeccable gardens. Not finding Ryan there, Will next headed to the local school, which housed elementary, middle, and high schools in different sections of the rambling concrete and masonry building. In the baseball field behind the school, Will found Ryan, who was tossing a tennis ball for Hank over and over again. Each time Hank would bring back the ball, tongue lolling, tail swaying, and golden fur bouncing. They repeated this over a dozen times as Will watched before Ryan finally pronounced that he was tired and plopped on the grass. Hank happily splayed out next to him, enjoying the cool grass on his belly and having not a care in the world so long as he had his matched person and his tennis ball.

Looking at the perfect golden retriever, Will asked Ryan whether he had any idea what a young GenDog pup like Hank had cost Ryan's parents. Ryan thought and said he did not know, but from a comment that Ryan's father made he thought it cost about the same as what his parents had paid for a new deck, which he knew had run about $12,000. Upon hearing this answer Will lamented "I was afraid of that. It would be about a quarter of what my parents brought in from the tree harvest last Christmas. This means that, even with steady business growth, a GenDog is never going to happen for me."

"Well come on, don't just sit there moping," responded Ryan. "You can always help me play with Hank," tossing Will the tennis ball. Will stood up and heaved the ball as far as he could down the field. Hank looked quickly to Ryan for permission and then tore off to retrieve the ball, bringing it back to Ryan even though it had been thrown by Will. Ryan tossed the ball again and Hank watched it so intently as he loped to catch it that he was oblivious to a squirrel that had been running across the field and froze directly under the dog as it leaped up gracefully, caught the ball mid-air, and pivoted to return to Ryan. Hank was exactly as programmed, loyal only to Ryan, focused on retrieving and gentle. Any trace of hip dysplasia that plagued the breed in prior years had been carefully edited out, and Hank would remain the perfect friend for many decades to come. After some time, Ryan suggested they get some lunch, and they headed to his house for BLT sandwiches, watermelon, and Oreo cookies. Will gratefully ate his fill but slipped a couple of pieces of bacon off his sandwich and into his pocket before saying he needed to head back.

Back at the old stump in the woods above his house, Will did not initially see Hunter. "Hey buddy, I bought you a treat," Will announced as he laid the bacon onto his observation rock. He suspected that the odor of salty, greasy meat would lure out the pup, and before too long he was not disappointed. "Hey there, little guy! It is good to see you again! Hungry?" said Will as the young dog poked his head out of the brush. "Do you mind if I call you Hunter? And even though I bet you are a really good hunter, maybe you would like a snack?" Come on over here," Will beckoned, waving the bacon in the air. But the dog did not budge, so Will laid the bacon back down and thought he better give Hunter some space.

Will walked off a bit, and even though it was slow and moving away from the stump, the dog yanked its head back and disappeared. Creating more distance, with the juicy treat now between Will and the stump, Will again beckoned to the dog. "It's OK, help yourself. I won't hurt you." He once more saw a nose come out of the brush at the base of the stump, sniffing and sniffing in the air. "That's it! Come on now. Tell you what, I won't even pay attention to you." Will squatted down and started picking small, juicy blackberries off of the thin vines that snaked their way along the ground, seeming to grow everywhere that there was a bit of sun. "See, I am just getting a snack too. I like these little berries. They might be small, but oh, they are so sweet."

Will kept talking quietly as he gradually popped berries into his mouth, staining his fingers a deep purple. He had learned from his mother to favor the wild blackberries, even though they were tiny compared to the big berries that could be found in abundance on the thorny canes of invasive Evergreen and Himalayan blackberry plants. The berries burst with intense flavor in his mouth, and Will appeared to be fully occupied. But he watched the dog out of the corner of his eye and was gratified to see Hunter slowly creep out of the brush and to the wonderful smelling bacon. As the dog wolfed his treat, they both heard the shrill cry of a raptor passing overhead. Hunter immediately bolted for cover and Will looked up to spot the white head of a large bird soaring on the currents above them, circling and looking for its next meal.

"Don't worry Hunter, you are kind of big for that bald eagle," said Will toward the tangle of green at the base of the stump. "Would you come back out please?" But it seemed that without the enticement of a snack, the dog was staying secreted. "I will bring you some more goodies tomorrow," said Will, as he prepared to ride off for home. "Will you remember me? I sure hope so."

Chapter 6

"How was Ryan today?" Emma asked Will at dinner. "Great!" answered Will. "We played fetch with Hank until both of us had tired throwing arms. Man, that dog loves to chase a ball. The weird part is that he almost ran over a squirrel and never even noticed."

"That never would have happened with the dogs we had when I was growing up" noted Dan. "They could smell a squirrel-like you and I smell bacon frying up in the morning. When they took out the gene for hip dysplasia in GenDog retrievers they must have edited out some sort of hunting gene."

"Speaking of hunting, I saw Hunter again today," said Will.

"Hunter? Who is that?" replied Dan.

"You remember, don't you?" answered Will. "That dog I found up in the clear cut? He came out for a snack."

"That darn dog again!" exploded Dan uncharacteristically. "I told you – leave that dog alone! Nobody is allowed to have or harbor a wild dog. And we are not going to be those people! We have enough trouble keeping food on the table without adding a bunch of legal issues! Now NO MORE!"

Will was stunned – it was very rare for his father to holler like that. Maybe their money problems were worse than he thought? But just like that, his Mom changed his thinking on the point, stunning him in the process.

"Dan, I hear that you can buy an 'orphaned' GenDog whose matched human has died unexpectedly. I think they cost a lot less than a GenDog pup. Maybe we should look into buying an orphaned GenDog for Will?" suggested Emma.

"Wow, that would be great!" Will said excitedly. "Can we Dad?"

"Will, I looked into that," answered Dan. "I know how much you have been longing for a dog. I looked it up on-line, and an orphaned GenDog still costs about half of a GenDog pup. So even if we could find an orphaned Gen-Dog that was the right age for you, I am afraid we still cannot afford that right now. Plus, I have heard rumors that GenDogs don't bond to a replacement person like they did their original matched human."

Deflated, Will pushed green beans around on his plate, thinking about how complicated the GenDog system must be. What if a GenDog died early, like if it was hit by a car? He supposed someone wealthy enough for a GenDog might just buy another one. Would it be the same as the first? And what about those orphaned GenDogs? "Mom, what happens to an orphaned GenDog if nobody wants it?" Emma looked at Dan for a few moments, but then simply said "I don't know Will. I think someone would want them."

"But," will persisted, "if an orphaned GenDog does not bond well to a new owner, wouldn't someone who could afford a GenDog in the first place simply buys a new Gen-Dog? So then does whoever bred the orphaned GenDog originally take them back? Or does the family of the person who died keep them? But if the family kept them, why would there be orphaned GenDogs for sale?"

Emma and Dan exchanged what to Will looked like sad looks, and Emma answered "I don't know. But it is not our worry, Will. Now finish your dinner." Will could not help but think there was more to be said on the topic, and he remained puzzled. But he knew not to push his luck and made a show of finishing his dinner.

Chapter 7

The next morning, Will smuggled a piece of French toast and a piece of sausage into his pocket at breakfast and headed out on his bike, leaving to the sound of his father's admonition to "leave that dog alone." But of course, Will did not do this, and instead pedaled his way up to Hunter's hiding spot by the old-growth stump. This time he did not need to wait long before he saw the familiar muzzle sneak its way out. "Good morning boy!" said Will. "At least I think you are a boy. Sorry to insult you if you are a girl!" Will pulled out the French toast, now cold and a little squished but still smelling good and eggy and sweet.

"Would you like some breakfast, Hunter?" Will was relieved to see that the dog did not run off when spoken to this time. But nor did it come further out of the brush. Will laid the French toast on a clean, warm spot on the rock that has become his visiting perch, and then backed off a few yards. Slowly the dog emerged, its hunger overcoming its natural fear. But the dog was limping a bit on its left front paw. "What's wrong there, Hunter? Come on now, get some food."

Will sat back on his haunches while Hunter made his way limping to the boulder, and then quickly scarfed the toast. Still sensing no threat, the dog more leisurely sniffed and licked every morsel and bit of grease it could find on the rock face. Will took this opportunity to creep towards the pup, which started to tense up but did not run. Will came slowly within a few feet of Hunter, then held out the chunk of sausage he had also stashed away. "Come on boy, are you still hungry? I have more for you, but this time you need to come all of the way to me."

Will held out the meaty morsel with an outstretched arm and was gratified to see Hunter make his way to him, stretching his neck to grab the sausage. "How was that, Hunter? Better than a mouse or whatever you have been eating, isn't it?" Hunter licked and savored every bit of grease on Will's hand, tail wagging slowly. "That's it, good dog," Will said quietly while he slowly moved his other hand to rub behind one of the dog's ears. "Oh wow, your fur is so soft! And I see you are a boy – I was right!" The delicious treat and gentle rubbing were more than Hunter could take, and soon his tail was swishing energetically back and forth while the pup licked Will's face and whined excitedly.

"Hey there Hunter, glad to meet you! Do you like your name, Hunter? I know you sure like my breakfasts!" Hunter could not seem to get enough petting and rubbing from Will, and Will noted that the dog was very thin under his fur. But that fur – it was the deep brown of fir tree bark on Hunter's back, transitioning to the gorgeous gold of sun-bleached hay down the dog's chest. Will likewise could not get enough of feeling the soft, warm fuzz of Hunter's back, though the dog's hind end was also carrying many burrs. It seemed to Will that petting this dog filled some empty spot inside him that he did not even know existed.

Crouched and reaching down the leg that Hunter was favoring, Will lifted a paw, which seemed huge compared to the rest of the young dog. Examining it carefully, he noted soft, downy fur growing between calloused leather-like paw pads, and found a small chunk of blackberry vine entwined in the fur at one spot. The local blackberry vines snaked their way along the ground, like thin low-strung barbed wire and frequently tripped Will up. If they hit a boot, no problem, but on a bare ankle, their bite could be painful. He didn't imagine that it could feel much better for Hunter. After some time, with a bit of tug of war from Hunter who was not 100% sure of things, Will was able to loosen the thorny debris and free it from Hunter's paw. "There you go boy, try that!" said Will as he released the paw. Hunter tested his paw and then excitedly danced about. A grateful dog jumped up with his front paws on Will's shoulders, knocking the boy over. "OK, OK, I get it, we are friends now!" said Will, laughing as the dog gave him sloppy kisses with an impossibly drooly tongue.

"What do you say, boy. Want to come home with me?" asked Will. Hunter seems ready to stick with the boy, so Will mounted his bicycle, slapped his thigh, and rode a bit in circles to see if the dog would follow him. Indeed, it seemed the bicycle did not trouble Hunter at all, and the dog followed Will along. Hunter easily trotted next to the bike as Will made his way down the hill, talking and whistling the whole time. "That a boy Hunter! Wait until you see where we are going! There is more food than you will know what to do with! Come on now!"

Will made it to the logging road that he would follow home, and all was going well. But then Hunter spied a doe with a white speckled fawn browsing grass that grew along the side of the road, and the dog was off like a shot. "No, Hunter! Come back here boy!" yelled Will, pedaling as fast as he could after his new friend, who could move. But the deer and dog quickly disappeared into thick woods, and Will had no hope of keeping up. "Hunter! Come here boy!" hollered Will, over and over again.

Will waited and called and paced for close to an hour, but there was no sign of the dog. "What if I never find him again?" Will thought dejectedly. "What if Hunter cannot make it back to his lair by the old stump? Maybe instead of rescuing Hunter, I put him into an unsafe position. A four-by-four could run him over. Or a cougar could catch him. Oh, I sure wish he would come back." Will beat himself up in his mind, worried sick as twilight started to fall. He finally had to admit defeat and headed home.

Will was unusually quiet at dinner that night. "Will, are you coming down with something?" asked Emma with concern. "No, I am just tired" answered Will, afraid to explain to his parents what was troubling him. "I might just go read in bed tonight if that is OK." And with that, Will excused himself and left two puzzled parents, who could not remember the last time Will voluntarily declared bedtime.

Chapter 8

"Well, you certainly seem to be feeling better," said Emma as she served Will seconds of pancakes and bacon the next morning. "Oh yes, Mom, thanks. Plus, your blueberry pancakes are so good!" replied Will, discretely wrapping a fat pancake around three crisp slices of bacon and tucking that inside his shirt while Emma was turned to the stove. "I plan on riding up in the clear cut all morning if that is OK with you. Could I take a couple of sandwiches with me?" Before long Will loaded his backpack with two peanut butter and honey sandwiches on whole wheat – his family's go-to meal for outdoor activities because it did not require refrigeration and tasted so good when you had worked up an appetite. He threw in an apple, some beef jerky, and a large bottle of water for good measure.

Worried still that some harm had come to his new friend, Will was relieved to see Hunter standing at the side of the logging road, wagging his tail and dancing around with excitement. "You must have been keeping a lookout for me boy. I sure am happy to see you again!" Will was gratified that Hunter was excited to see him – even before he brought any food out. But when he handed over the pancake and bacon strips, Hunter could hardly contain himself. "Slow down there boy, it's not going anywhere!" It did not take long for the dog to dispatch all offered food. Hunter then rolled over on his back, exposing his belly and wiggling his body into C-shapes from side to side. "Oh, so you want a belly rub, do you?"

And soon enough Hunter was pretty much ecstatic, with a full stomach and a rubbed belly. Will marveled at how soft the dog's belly felt. It was mostly bare of fur, except for a fine down. Just as he was bending low to the task, Hunter pushed Will playfully with his back legs, sending the boy sprawling on his backside in the dirt. Just as quickly Hunter sprang up and started licking Will around the face and ears, while Will shrieked with joy. The two wrestled in this way like a couple of pups that they were for a good hour or so.

After a time, Will thought he would see what Hunter thought of his bicycle. The boy hopped on and pedaled off, calling the dog to follow. Hunter thought this was a grand new game, and loped in circles around Will as the boy pedaled around. Every once in a while, the dog would run off after something that he scented, but he always returned. The dog's natural athleticism was amazing. He could leap over huge downed logs with ease, or up onto a stump as if it was no trouble at all. Hunter then would look back at Will as if to ask "Are you coming?"

In this way Will and Hunter whiled away the morning, exploring together as they became a team. The duo wandered their way down to a stream at one point, and soon were both splashing around. Will caught small trout fingerlings in his hands and showed one to Hunter. Cupping the wiggling young brown and green fish gently in his hands, Will held the squirming fish up to Hunter. He thought Hunter would merely sniff it but the dog grabbed and swallowed it whole. "Whoa Hunter, let's let these little guys get bigger, why don't we? But maybe you are hungry?"

Thoroughly wet and cooled off, Will clambered back up from the stream to a sunny spot and settled down for lunch, with Hunter sprawled happily at his feet. He pulled out the sandwiches to share with the dog. Will had always loved the way that the honey made a crystallized crust inside the sandwich between the peanut butter and the bread. Each bite gave layers of soft bread, creamy peanut butter, and crisp honey. He never became tired of this meal, maybe because it always accompanied a hiking, biking, or snowshoeing adventure. Just a taste of the simple meal reminded him of past adventures. But the sandwich that Will gave to Hunter seemed to remind the pup only how much he loved food. Hunter was only too happy to eat his sandwich and part of Will's.

At the end of the day, Hunter followed Will down to the cabin. "Hey buddy, you will need to stay in here, OK?" said Will, showing Hunter to the inside of the family's barn. "I can't show you to my parents yet, but you will be warm here, and I can bring you food." Somehow Hunter seemed to understand and curled up on top of a small stack of straw bales that were sitting on a pallet on the floor. Gnawing on some jerky Will left him, Hunter watched the boy with some concern as he backed out of the barn and closed the door.

Chapter 9

"Are your pants getting short?" Emma asked Will. "You have been eating like a horse these last few weeks. I suppose you have hit a growth spurt and we'll have to take you shopping for new jeans and boots before school starts."

Will did not know if he was growing but sure could tell that Hunter was, and felt bad about all the food he had been smuggling to the barn. "Umm, well, maybe. But that would be expensive, wouldn't it? Can I work in the garden with you to earn money to pay for some good boots?"

Before long Will was digging his hands into the warm earth of the family's garden, pulling up weeds that stole water from the tomato plants. Every time he brushed the stem of the plants, he caught a whiff of green tomato scent that also permeated his hands. He noted that the tomatoes were turning red finally. It appeared that they would win the annual Northwest summer battle to produce ripe tomatoes before fall rains started that led to blighted plants. "Mom, these tomatoes are kind of wrinkly. And we get so few at the end of the season before the weather turns. Why bother?"

"Will, go get one of the tomatoes we have inside the kitchen for sandwich slicing." Will complied, and Emma said "Now try a bite of that. What do you taste?" Will tried a nibble and answered "Duh, tomato. Kind of mushy but not bad. It would be good with some bacon and lettuce on sourdough."

"Now pick one of those wrinkled red ones, and try a bite of that," instructed Emma. Will pulled a firm but yielding fruit from a plant. The tomato seemed impossibly dense and was a deep blood-red. He bit into the sun-warmed globe, which was shaped like a miniature pumpkin with deep creases separating lobes extending from the stem that came together into a dark scabby bit at the bottom. He could taste salty-sweet summer in the intensely flavorful juice. "Oh wow, this doesn't need bacon. Why don't the tomatoes you buy at the store taste this good?" asked Will as he savored every bit of the tomato, chunky red juice dripping down his chin.

"We let our tomatoes ripen fully on the vine. We don't treat them with anything so sometimes they get holes from bugs," answered Emma. "People want to buy fruit that looks perfect. So most store-bought fruit are likely sprayed with some sort of insecticide. I try to buy organic ones when I can find and afford them. But whether or not organic, commercial tomatoes have been bred to be firm so that they don't bruise during shipment. Not only that but they are picked partially green so that they are firm when shipped. They then are forcibly ripened with some sort of gas or may finish ripening on the shelf, but they just cannot capture the sun the way ours do." Will thought the mealy pink fruit from the store they had been eating all summer should be called something besides "tomatoes" because they bore little resemblance to the luscious red fruit he had just eaten. He now viewed the tomato plants with new understanding and reverently made sure that no weeds would cheat them of water or nutrients.

As they were finishing work for the day, Will volunteered to put the garden trowels away in the barn. "You seem to be finding an awful lot of reasons to go to the barn lately," said Emma. "Just trying to help," answered Will. After the boy had stashed the gear away, which took an unusually long time, he headed inside to wash up for dinner. Emma collected the days' eggs, walked to the barn, and opened the sliding door. She saw something move in the back of the barn, disappearing behind the pile of straw bales. With a knowing smile, Emma selected two eggs and left them on top of the bales, and quietly left, closing the door securely behind her.

"It bothers me that we cannot get Will the dog that he wants," said Dan as he climbed into bed. "He has everything he needs, but sometimes it is nice to have a little of what you want. Maybe I made a mistake having us start this tree farm. It has been seven years and we are just now breaking even."

"Remember, Dan, why we decided to live and work here," replied Emma, snuggling into the crook of Dan's arm and laying her head on his chest. "We were both pretty stressed and running ourselves ragged with our Seattle jobs. We worked so hard just to be able to afford an apartment there. I couldn't see Will growing up in that sea of concrete, and we would both have had to continue to work full time at our office jobs, with Will in day school. We might be strapped now, but at least we know who we are here in the woods. And you know that boy loves all the freedom he has to explore here."

Emma drew closer still, saying "Besides, I have a feeling everything is going to work out. Now let's get some sleep, we have a busy day tomorrow." Dan was not sure what to make of Emma's premonition. But the covers were warm and, hugging Emma close, he soon nodded off.

Upstairs in his room, it had been fifteen minutes or so since Will heard his parents milling about downstairs, and he was fairly confident that they had turned in for the night. He slowly opened his bedroom door, hoping the hinge did not squeak. Hearing nothing, Will padded his way along the hall and crept down the stairs, avoiding the third stair from the top and its inevitable creak. His parents' room was indeed all quiet, and Will silently left out the back door and went to the barn.

He opened the barn door and softly whistled. Seeming instantly Hunter was at the door, leaping up with his paws on Will's chest. "Whoa boy, you must have been waiting for me! OK, settle down now. We are going to try something new tonight." Will rubbed behind Hunter's ears, with the dog melting into a puddle of wriggling, relaxed fur. "We have to be quiet now, and stick close, OK?"

Will walked back to the house, Hunter dancing around him excitedly, wondering what this new game might be. Reaching the porch, Will shushed Hunter, blowing across a finger with pursed lips. "Stay right with me boy," whispered Will. He led Hunter the long way through the living room so that the click-click of the pup's claws would be muffled by the carpet, and avoided the hallway outside his parent's room. They then crept back up the stairs and into Will's room, closing the door behind them.

–

"What is bothering you, Dan?" said Emma one night later that week. "You have been tossing and turning for hours. Why don't you curl in and get some sleep with me?"

"It just bothers me that we cannot afford everything we would like to give Will. His bicycle is a hand-me-down from your sister's kids. And even something as basic as a dog, which should be pretty simple for a kid living in the country, is out of our reach." Dan continued to fret as he rolled over again in bed, sleep continuing to elude him.

"We had a lot more cash at our old jobs," reminded Emma. "But we hardly saw each other, let alone had any time for a child. And would you want Will to grow up in the city? At least here he has all that he needs, plus trees to climb, hillsides to explore, streams to investigate, and frogs to catch."

"Thanks, Emma, you know how to put into perspective," said Dan. "And I have to admit, Will does seem pretty happy. Is that offer of a cuddle still good?"

Meanwhile, upstairs, Will pulled back his covers and patted his bed. Hunter jumped right up and snuggled against Will, who pulled the covers over them both and fell contentedly to sleep.

Chapter 10

As Emma put her family's sheets into the wash, she noticed that there was a good amount of dog hair on Will's sheets. She smiled to herself but said nothing. Later that morning she left an old shedding comb for dogs she had kept from when she was a girl, as well as a bucket and a spare bottle of shampoo by the hay bale stack in the barn. She did not know if it was ideal that the shampoo was coconut scented, but did not think it would hurt anything.

"Will, come help me unload these sacks of chicken feed and scratch," said Dan as he hoisted a fifty-pound sack out of the truck bed and onto his shoulder. "I bought enough to last us all fall and almost to Christmas." Will hustled over with a wheelbarrow and slid a bag of scratch off the tailgate, which landed with a metallic thud in the wheelbarrow. He wasn't strong enough to lift a sack-like his Dad, but they had worked out a routine whereby he could shuttle sacks over to save Dan some trips.

More importantly, he wanted to make sure Hunter was well hidden in the barn. Dan dropped his first sack onto a pallet near the hay bales and turned to get another as Will wheeled the barrow over to the pallet storage area. As soon as Dan cleared the barn, Will gave a soft whistle under his breath and was rewarded by Hunter popping up from his snoozing spot, ready to play. "Not yet boy," whispered Will. The boy led Hunter to the other side of the barn and had him lay down behind some 55-gallon barrels. "Stay, Hunter. Do you understand? You need to Stay," Will whispered as he backed up. Luckily Hunter was a fast study and seemed to understand. The dog laid down with his head on his paws, eyebrow tufts raised and waited patiently.

Dan and Will made fast work of moving the feed, Will wheeling one sack for each that Dan carried and Dan then stacking both. Each time a sack was dropped, the sweet smell of grain puffed out, and it was enjoyable work. Will was feeling relieved that they were almost done and Hunter had not been discovered. He did not like hiding the truth from his parents but was glad he was getting away with it. At least he thought he was, still puzzled by the dog grooming supplies that magically appeared in the barn.

But on the last trip into the barn, there was a loud crash as Hunter knocked over a barrel and streaked between Will and Dan over to the pallets.

"What the heck! Will, is that the dog you were talking about?" shouted Dan as he nearly dropped a sack. "That better not be! You know we said you could not keep it!"

Instantly nearing tears at being yelled at, Will said "Come here, boy." Hunter, confused by the yelling he had never heard a human do, crept over slowly. "Dad, this is Hunter. I am sorry but he is a good dog and needed someone to help him find enough food." Hunter walked on over to Dan, tail low and swishing between his rear legs. The pup then dropped a fat mouse at Dan's feet, and sat back on his haunches, looking up expectantly at the beet red man.

"Wait, what's this?" asked Dan. "Did you catch a mouse?" Hunter wiggled his tail hopefully. "You say his name is Hunter? Well, I guess that is a good name for him, he sure caught this mouse. And we have no end of mice, always eating our grain."

"I was going to order some more traps, but I suppose you could help control things in the meantime," said Dan gruffly. "He can stay awhile, Will, but you know we cannot keep him. We will talk later about your disobeying us." Hunter seemed to sense that the ice had been broken with Dan, and shoved his head into the palm of the man's hand. Dan, surprised, tentatively stroked Hunter's head. "He is pretty friendly, isn't he?"

Chapter 11

Hunter's reprieve lasted for a week, and then a month, and then three months. The whole family had fallen for the pup, which was now a stretched-out but still skinny adolescent. He was a gorgeous, athletic dog, a bit ribby as he had not yet bulked up. But muscles visibly rippled under the fur on his chest. Every day Hunter followed Will into the woods to explore, jumping and racing about, often running off after some scent or other but always circling back to Will.

Around the cabin, Hunter seemed to always be underfoot as Dan and Emma went about doing their chores. "I have not seen a single sign of mice or rats in the chicken coop," Emma remarked. "Either have I," admitted Dan. "That mutt is sure earning his keep. But I am not looking forward to how sad Will is going to be when the dog is finally gone." While talking, Dan, seemingly without knowing he was doing so, slowly rubbed Hunter's ears.

"Do we need to turn him in, Dan?" asked Emma. "We could just let him stay. He sure is good company for Will, and I do feel better knowing Will has company while he is out roaming who knows where."

"Come on Emma, you know we talked about this. There is no way we could afford the fine for harboring this dog. It's fine to be sentimental, but it is our job to keep this family safe and we cannot do that if we cannot buy the supplies that we need and pay the mortgage on this place. We agreed, now don't make me the bad guy." As he said this, Dan seemed to catch himself and pulled his hand away from Hunter. The thought of turning Hunter into the authorities bothered him, but he knew he had to protect his family and stay strong. Unless perhaps they could drop Hunter off in the woods far away from their cabin? The dog certainly knew how to hunt, he would make it, wouldn't he? Dan continued to muse about this, sure that he needed to see the dog go but wrestling with himself as to the best way.

Emma, who had seen how close Dan was also becoming to Hunter, simply said nothing. She knew her man well, including the tender marshmallow that lived inside that gruff exterior.

"I will just be a few minutes while I find some parts," said Dan to Will as they pulled up to the hardware store. Dan carefully parked his old Ford crew cab pickup, which made a manly diesel rumble when running, in the shade under a tree on the edge of the parking lot. The truck was blue-green, much like that of deep ocean water, though its original sticker called the paint "Forest Green", and a white aluminum bed canopy kept things secure and dry. "Wait here and keep Hunter in the canopy in the back, OK?"

Will was only too happy to listen, as this was the first time that he had ever been able to take Hunter to town. On the roads leading to town, Will had ridden with Hunter in the bed of the pickup. Will had dangled his legs off the open tailgate, one hand braced on the pick-up body and the other wrapped around his dog in case they happened to pass a deer. They both loved the green smells of the forest passing by them in the breeze, speaking mysteries of moss and hollows begging to be explored. After carefully winding his way down along the gravel road to town, Dan had pulled over, shut Hunter in the canopied bed, and had Will climb into the cab with a seat belt before they hit the paved main road into town.

Everything was going well at the hardware store until Karen McProbis spied Will in the pickup. The frumpy middle-aged woman had assigned herself the task of keeping track of everyone in town. She was a de facto, one-person news reporter and gossip columnist for the town's non-existent newspaper, the function of which was met by a community Facebook page. "Well hello Will, I have not seen you in town for months. What's been keeping you busy?"

"Hi, Mrs. McProbis. I have just been helping my folks with the tree farm and spending lots of time with school work. That's all," responded Will, glancing in the rear-view mirror with the hope that Hunter would stay down low in the truck bed.

"But normally you go in with your Dad to get some of that free popcorn that is always popped in the store. Are you feeling OK? I just never knew you to be content sitting down when there was fun and food to be had. Maybe you are keeping guard on some tools in the back of the truck?" asked Mrs. McProbis, peering over Will's shoulder. The woman had a nose telling her something was different here, and she seemed reluctant to skip finding out what that something could be.

"Nope, just taking a break," Will replied. "Oh look, here comes my Dad. I guess we'll be going now. You take care of yourself, OK Mrs. McProbis?"

With that his Dad arrived and said "Hello Karen, how are you today?" At the sound of Dan's voice, Hunter could not contain himself. The dog jumped up, put his paws on the inside of the window of the canopy, rocking the truck, and let out a hearty "Woof!" that also sprayed drool on the canopy window.

"Well, well, what do you have here?" asked Mrs. McPro-bis. "Do you have a GenDog now Dan?"

"Umm, well, we have been discussing getting one," replied Dan. He looked down at his boots while trying to figure out how to settle the old biddie down while also not telling a lie and setting a bad example for Will.

"But wait a minute," said Mrs. McProbis, peering in through the canopy window at Hunter. "I have never seen a GenDog breed that looks like this. He is pretty big and his parts don't quite match. Why I would have to say this is a mutt. Which means it is not a GenDog. Tell me I am wrong, Dan."

"Well, no, you are not wrong Karen. But, well…"

"No buts Dan. You know it is illegal to have a mutt. We'll have to talk to CERT Animal Control about this. They'll take care of this pitiful creature and make sure it cannot dilute the GenDog bloodlines."

"Karen, we all know how Animal Control "takes care" of natural dogs, don't we? Doesn't it bother you to see loving animals put down?" replied Dan. Upon hearing this comment from inside the truck, Will blanched and stared at his Dad, silently pleading for help. At the same time, Hunter, oblivious to the discussion but thrilled to have people paying him attention, started thumping the inside of the truck bed with his tail, as his tongue lolled and he danced about.

Dan took a breath and made a decision. Sometimes the rules had to be bent, and he hoped Will would understand the transgression in truth he was about to commit. "But hold your horses anyway, Karen. This "mutt" as you call him is named Hunter, and yes, he is Will's dog. And he is legal." Will's eyes widened with surprise – he could keep the dog? Wow, this was turning out to be a great day. But how?

Will started to ask a question, but his father held up a hand to shush him. "You know that the CERT Act included a few exceptions. One of these was a grace period for existing natural dogs to live out their life spans."

"You cannot tell me this mutt was existing when CERT was passed, Dan. Why he is much too young." Fumed Mrs. McProbis.

"True, but let me finish. Another exception was a one-time right to clone an existing natural dog. You're looking at the clone of my parents' old dog, Roscoe. They loved that dog so much and, just before he passed, commissioned a clone. They are getting up in years but wanted Will to have the same experience with a great dog that they had, and also want to be able to visit it," explained Dan.

Will was really confused now but decided it was probably a good thing not to say anything. "So, Karen, you see that there is no call for contacting Animal Control. Now if you will excuse us, I need to get back to work. Have a good day." At this Mrs. McProbis let out a "harrumph" but backed off, and Dan climbed into his truck and started the engine.

As they pulled away, Will could not contain himself any longer. "Dad, what was that about Grandma and Grandpop? Did they have a dog named Roscoe? I sure don't remember that. And what about..."

"Settle down son," interrupted Dan. "Now, you know it is always important to tell the truth, right?"

"Yes," answered Will.

"Good," responded Dan. "That's important, and I live my life by that maxim, as should you. But sometimes there is a bigger issue, where telling the truth would do a lot of harm, and telling a lie would do no harm. And this is one of those cases."

"So, Grandma and Grandpop did not have a dog named Roscoe? And Hunter is not a clone? Do I still have to get rid of him?"

Dan gave Will a one-armed hug, drawing the boy into his side. "Well, let's just say that it looks like we have a resident mouse catcher. Keep Hunter on the down low, and we'll see how it goes." Will looked back through the rear window into the canopy and smiled at the goofy dog with the lolling tongue, and thought it was about the finest day he could remember.

Chapter 12

The long, rangy dog leaped out from the bushes and chased alongside Will as he pedaled his way home from school. This had become their daily routine that fall. Hunter had stretched out but had the long, gangly build of a teenager. The dog could run circles around Will and, growing impatient, would frequently detour off to chase a chipmunk that chee-chee-cheed from atop a tree or a grouse that set to flight from the brush with wings whirring. Always Hunter would circle back to touch base with Will, the dog's tongue-lolling, the boy standing on his pedals and grinning, as they made their way uphill to the family cabin.

The air was crisp with fall, and piles of large, golden-red leaves from big leaf maple trees crinkled under Will's tires. He pedaled past an old apple tree, noting that the lowest branches were broken and stripped of fruit. This sight reminded Will to call out "Hey bear bear, hey bear bear!" as he rode along, not wanting to surprise any black bear feasting in preparation for winter. Large piles of bear scat had been evident on the roads home all summer. Earlier they were purple-hued and seedy from eating berries, but now that apples were in season, they were reddish-orange and full of skin bits. Hunter had to stop and smell each pile deeply, deciphering information about the creature that had deposited it about which Will could only guess.

Hunter sometimes made Will's heart catch when the dog crashed through the woods. Instinctively Will would freeze when he heard such a noise, thinking that it might be a large bear, wild cat, or coyote. But every time the noise would be followed by a goofy-grinned muzzle as Hunter returned from his latest chase.

That day Will's instinct proved to be good, as he came around a corner and saw a small bear, a yearling that was one of last year's cubs, ambling along. On hearing Will's "Bear, bear" call, the bear stopped, turned, and stood up on its hind legs as it sniffed at the boy and dog. "Hey now Mr. Bear, we don't mean any harm. You can have all the apples you want," said Will calmly as he came to a standstill. Hunter, while now fairly large, was still a pup at heart. The dog skidded to a stop and then turned and hid behind Will. Hunter pushed his nose and front end between Will's legs, facing the bear. Will felt the dog's warm, soft fur on the inside of his legs and drew a measure of comfort; they were standing together, come what may, and he would do what he could to protect Hunter. "It's OK Hunter," whispered Will. "He'll leave us alone as long as we leave him alone." Then in a calm voice, he continued "Hey Mr. Bear, you're OK, don't worry about us. We'll leave you alone, go on your way now." The bulky bear dropped back down, huffed back and forth, and then seemed satisfied. Its deep black fur glistening in the sun, the bear sauntered into the woods, leaving behind an earthy scent trail smelling of fruit mixed with the punky wood and decayed wildlife in which the animal must have been digging.

Will settled for a while to make sure the animal was good and gone, his heart gradually slowing from hummingbird speed to something closer to that of a tortoise. "Wow Hunter, I sure am glad that you were here," laughed Will once the bear was well out of sight. "Good to see you had my back – literally, you big scaredy-cat! Well, I guess you are still a pup. Come on, let's go home."

The pair continued the ride, but Will could not help but look over his shoulder every few minutes to make sure they were not followed.

Hunter sat on the floor next to the table, hoping some stray bits of the chicken that the family was enjoying made it his way. "I saw a bear on the road home today," commented Will as he helped himself to a crispy drum stick. "I think it was one of the cubs we spotted last year, but it is getting to be a pretty good size now."

"Hunter was with you, right?" asked Dan. After his initial reluctance, Dan had taken a shine to the dog. He reached down and absently scratched behind Hunter's ear, thinking how glad he was that they had a dog to keep

Will safe during his wanderings. Hunter loved the rubs, but the spots of drool under the dog's jowls demonstrated that food would be even more welcome.

"Well, he was," answered Will. "But Hunter hid behind me when we saw the bear."

"Oh well, I guess he has some more growing up to do yet," chuckled Dan. "Hopefully if you ever really need him to protect you, he will rise to the occasion. Isn't that right, Hunter?" The big dog thumped his tail in response, having not understood a word other than his name, and hopeful this would mean a taste of the wonderful smelling dinner.

Emma was just glad that Will had a friend, and passed a scrap of chicken skin to the dog under the table. The rule was that Hunter could only have scraps after the family was done eating, but this seemed to be a rule that all members of the family broke when no one was looking.

"Ryan invited me to go watch him do an agility trial with Hank tomorrow," said Will. Is it OK if I go and take Hunter?"

Dan exchanged a nervous look with Emma, but then paused and drew a long breath. "I suppose so, Son. But remember that people must not find out that Hunter is a natural dog. No one can know, not even Ryan." Dan again had a moment of disquiet about the wisdom of essentially asking his son to lie, and worried what this would mean in the future. But Hunter had become too big a part of Will's life, and frankly all of their lives, to risk losing him.

Chapter 13

Not a hair was out of place in the immaculately groomed coats of the dogs waiting for their turns at the agility trial on the high school field. Will spotted Ryan and Hank, the dog's long golden fur shining in the low fall sunlight. One-by-one the owners took their dogs through the course, with the well-trained animals weaving through poles, running through tunnels, and traveling over bridges with ease.

When it was Ryan and Hank's turn, Will cheered on his friend. The dog was laser-focused, ignoring other dogs, as it ran the course, spurred by the commands of Ryan. Each time Hank completed a task, Ryan rewarded him with a bit of hot dog drawn from a pouch at the boy's waist.

Will thought the agility trials looked like fun, though he was somewhat bored by the long wait between events. He laid back in the grass, looking up at the passing clouds, and waited for Ryan to finish. Hunter in the meantime had other pursuits in mind and roamed the border of the field looking for critters.

At one point he started digging furiously under a root, on the hunt for a field mouse. Hunter kicked up bits of grass and dirt, which happened to hit Mrs. McProbis as she walked by with a highly groomed poodle on a leash. She jerked her dog back so that no soil would get on the shaved puffs of fur.

"You cannot have a dog off-leash here!" shouted Mrs. McProbis in Will's direction. "Didn't you read the signs posted at the entry to the field?" Will jumped up and whistled for Hunter, who came loping over, dancing around and thinking it was time to play.

"I am sorry Mrs. McProbis, Hunter did not mean any harm," said Will as he passed the loop of a leash over Hunter's neck. Hunter pulled back for a moment, unused to the restraint, but stilled once Will reached down and rubbed the dog's head. "He is still a pup and just needs to run."

"Nevertheless, you must keep that dog under control. I just don't see why your grandmother would have cloned such an odd-looking mutt. And how did you end up with it, anyway?" asked Mrs. McProbis.

"He's not odd looking!" retorted Will, hauling Hunter off and dodging Mrs. McProbis' question. They sat back down in the grass, with Hunter pulling on the lead every time something interesting went by. Soon they were joined by Ryan and Hank, who had finished their first agility run. The retriever lay next to Ryan, elegant and obedient as an oversized plush toy. Will could not help comparing Hunter, fur stained and nose browned with dirt, dancing on the lead and straining to go and play, to the self-restraint and polish of Hank. Hunter was a lot of work in such a civilized setting. But in his heart Will knew that like most things that came imperfectly and with effort, his furry friend had the greater true value.

"That's him, officer," said Mrs. McProbis in the background, pointing toward Will and Ryan's group. "Have you ever seen a cloned dog like that? I cannot even tell what breeds he might be. Should that be allowed?"

The CERT agent, sporting a name badge that said "RUDEY", came over and appraised Hunter, who luckily had finally settled down in one spot. Will put a protective arm around Hunter and asked why the officer was there. "I am told your dog is a clone, Son. Is that correct? He does not look like any dog I have seen in recent years," said the agent as he eyed the mixed coloration of Hunter's fur.

Will responded as his father had told him. "Yes sir, we are sure he is a clone. My grandparents loved their last dog, Roscoe, so they cloned him."

"But your dog looks like a pup. How could he be so young?"

"Well, Roscoe was not much more than a pup himself when CERT was passed. And he lived a long life, something like 16 years old. They just had him cloned last year."

"And why do you have him," continued the officer suspiciously.

"You can see that Hunter is a pretty big boy. My Gramps and Gram are getting pretty old, and don't want to get knocked down."

"But then why clone him at all?" pressed the CERT agent.

"I guess they just wanted me to have a dog that was as good as Roscoe. And Hunter IS a really good dog," responded Will as Hunter rolled over and exposed his dirty belly.

"If everything that the boy says is true, Karen, there is no violation here," said the Officer finally.

"But just look at the beast!" said Mrs. McProbis heatedly. "Why, he is a filthy mess and all sorts of odd-looking. Have you ever seen a dog that looked like that?"

"She has a point, son. Exactly what breed is your dog? You know that we will have to take him if he is a natural dog, don't you?"

Will thought fast of all of the breeds he knew, trying desperately to explain Hunter. His Dad had only said he thought Hunter was a "Heinz 57" breed, and Will could not figure out what ketchup had to do with his dog. "I am not sure exactly. But I think he is part Rottweiler, part German Shepard, and part something else."

"We don't allow mongrels nowadays. But it sounds like your dog snuck in under the wire," said the officer. "Just keep an eye on him, would you? We cannot have mutts propagating."

"Will do, Officer," answered Will as he hauled Hunter off. He did not know what "prop gating" was, but was pretty sure that it was a skill his dog did not have.

Mrs. McProbis continued to glare at Hunter as he was led away, leaving Will with an uneasy feeling.

Chapter 14

Christmas day dawned bright and cold. Snow was a rarity at Christmas in the Hood Canal region of Washington, and it was no surprise that this day would not be white. However, it was at least not raining, and Will woke up excited that it was a crisp winter day. While it had grown cool in the cabin over the night, the boy was snug in bed with Hunter curled up against his legs. Noting that it seemed to be a little light out, or at least if he imagined hard enough he thought he saw signs of dawn, Will hoped it was not too early to be up. "Come on boy, let's go see what Santa brought!"

Will crept by his parents' room so as not to wake them, and then bounded down the stairs with Hunter following by his side. His parents had left the Christmas tree lights on, and the multi-colored glow revealed a decent pile of brightly wrapped packages under the tree. Will snooped through these, hefting a few and shaking others. He was initially disappointed because none seemed to have the size or weight that would match the pellet rifle that he had hoped and asked for, putting it at the top of his wish list. He knew it would not be a real rifle, but he wanted one regardless to plunk at targets and play the outdoorsman. Regardless of whether his wish was fulfilled, it was hard to remain disappointed Christmas morning, with the tree and the lights and lots of boxes that surely held good things.

He opened his stocking and played with the goodies that it contained, waiting for his parents to wake up. A yo-yo, some playing cards, and three tiny-scale matchbox cars. Will's stocking also included his favorite Pocky sticks, a Japanese cookie stick dipped in chocolate, strawberry, or banana coating, as well as individual serving-sized boxes of sweet cereals he was not usually allowed to have, like Captain Crunch and Lucky Charms. Will munched on sweets and occasionally shared a bite with Hunter, who seemed to have developed a sweet tooth but never received enough of these treats to cause him any harm.

When Will's parents came down, they each grabbed their stocking, leaving one extra on the fireplace mantel. Will gave it a puzzled look, and then glanced at his Mom. "It seems Santa left Hunter a stocking," said Emma. "Why don't you help him open it?"

Wow, thought Will, Hunter is part of the family! He pulled down the stocking and found a squeaky ball that he tossed to Hunter, who chomped on it repeatedly to give a satisfying series of squeaks. He handed Hunter another gift-wrapped item that was oddly meaty-smelling, and the dog tore into the paper. Once Will saw that it was a pack of chicken jerky, he snagged the interior plastic envelope and pulled out a piece for Hunter, who could not believe his good fortune.

It seemed to take his Mom forever to finish making biscuits and gravy for breakfast, which was served with fresh Ruby Red grapefruit halves. While it was their tradition and food that he loved, Will knew that they could not open presents until after the meal. He wolfed the flaky biscuits smothered by creamy gravy and little bits of sausage, making sure to save a bite for Hunter as did each of his parents. Soon enough the table was cleared and the excited anticipation could be quenched.

The family took turns exchanging gifts, though as usual there were many more presents for Will than his parents. Will was most excited to watch his father open the wooden woodpecker that he had carved out of a chunk of cedar, the head painted with a red cap and white and black side stripes, and a black back like the large pileated woodpeckers he had seen in the forest. For his mother, with the help of his father as Will was not yet allowed to use power tools, he had made a birdhouse to hang on a tree outside the cabin. It was brightly painted green with a red roof.

His parents were thrilled with their gifts, and Will was happy to receive a new baseball mitt and a small backpack that he could carry when riding his mountain bike. He also received some new jeans and socks, but it was hard to show enthusiasm for those. Overall, it was a very good

Christmas, even though Will could not help but feel a little deflated over the lack of a pellet gun. Perhaps next year when things were not so tight.

"Dad, did you want to go play some catch?" asked Will.

"Why sure son. Though your Mom was better at softball than I was at baseball," answered Dan. "Maybe she will join us?"

"I would be happy too! After we are finished opening gifts," replied Emma, with a wink to Dan.

Will was puzzled, looking around and seeing no other gifts under the tree. "What do you mean Mom? I think we are done, aren't we?"

Emma turned and reached behind the couch, pulling out a ball of twine that was partially unrolled to yield a length of twine snaking along the back wall of the living room and disappearing into the hallway. "Maybe you better see where this goes," said Emma as she handed the ball to Will.

Will was not sure what was going on but figured it must be something good. He started winding the twine onto the ball and was soon out of the living room, down the hall, through the kitchen, and out the back door. He followed the twine below a large rock. He found a single key tied to the twine, which continued on its way across the yard. "What is this, Mom?" asked Will.

"Gee, I guess you will just have to follow it to find out." Will started again, and followed the twine across the yard, around the base of a maple tree, then heading back to the side of the cabin, where it wrapped around a water spigot and took off again in the opposite direction. Will followed the twine, zig-zagging around the yard and under the porch until finally, he followed it to behind the woodshed.

And there he found an honest-to-goodness motorcycle! A shiny red Honda 125 dirt bike! Oh man, could this be for him? "Mom, Dad, is this mine?"

"It sure is, Son," answered Emma. "We received a nice price for the trees this year," said Dan. "You worked hard helping us, and someone we knew up in Port Angeles was selling his kid's bike. You deserve it – Merry Christmas, Will."

Practically vibrating with excitement, Will stood the bike up off the kickstand and pushed it out from behind the woodshed. He had learned how to ride a motorbike by trying out Ryan's 80 cc Honda dirt bike, so he knew he could handle this bike even if it was larger. It might not be brand new, but it was an even bigger bike than Ryan had – for once he could show off something he had to Ryan! "Can I try this now?" Will asked his parents.

"First you better go check in the hall closet," answered Emma. "And put on your work boots, gloves, and a jacket."

Will raced inside to the closet, Hunter running along excited by the activity but not understanding where Will was going. Inside the closet, Will found a shiny red helmet that fit his head just perfectly. "Come on boy, let's go!"

The bike started up easily, and Will rode it in slow circles around the cabin, getting the feel of the clutch. After a few laps, he felt ready to take it up the logging road to the clear cut. At first, Hunter seemed puzzled by the noise that the bike made, and hung back a bit. But as Will accelerated, shifting from first to second, it suddenly dawned on the dog that his boy was moving much faster than he could usually do on a bicycle.

Hunter sped up to keep time with Will and then shot out in front of the motorbike, running flat out down the road, tongue lolling and looking back every so often to see that the boy was indeed keeping up with him. Hunter ran with joyous abandon, alongside and in front of the motorcycle, ecstatic that someone could finally run fast with him. The dog's joy was infectious, and Will grinned from ear to ear. He had a sense now of what it meant to be wild and free, and alive. Not just existing, but truly living in that moment.

"You like running with motorcycles, don't you boy!" Sharing this sheer freedom with Hunter made him feel closer than ever to this wonderful, unconstrained dog. Every once in a while, Hunter would shoot off the road after something, not yet understanding that Will could not follow everywhere. As Will would pass the dog, he would whistle for Hunter, who would come crashing back out of the woods and rejoin Will.

Will and Hunter spent a fun morning in this fashion, stopping every so often at the creek so that Hunter could drink and rest. At lunchtime, the two were exhausted and happy, and the ham sandwiches and apples that Emma provided had never tasted so good.

Chapter 15

The bright February morning dawned cold and crisp. Hunter was sleeping curled up on a rug in front of the warm wood stove, having figured out the primal lure of the hearth. Will was excited to see a fresh layer of snow, with more falling. Six inches or more of fresh snow had built up on earth that had been frozen for the past week, so it was sticking around rather than melting as most often disappointedly happened in that area of the Olympic peninsula. After breakfast, the boy stepped outside and strapped on a pair of snowshoes that he had rarely been able to use. Will loved the way that every sound echoed in the frigid, dry air, and the latches on his snowshoes made a cracking noise like a stick breaking as he snapped on the straps. His snowshoes whispered down through the first few inches of snow each time he took a step.

"Come on Hunter, you will like this!" called Will as he popped his head back into the front door. Hunter stood, stretched, and wandered his way to the door. He poked his nose outside and took a sniff of the crisp air. The dog took a tentative step or two into the white fluff, then continued, shaking his paws after each step as he tried to figure out what was clinging to his fur.

After walking gingerly, and seeing Will progress on his snowshoes, Hunter decided that the snow was not bad at all. It was a lot of fun – and soon the dog was leaping about, bounding pogo-like, scooping up mouthfuls of snow and digging holes each time he smelled something of interest under the cool, fluffy blanket. Hunter had matured and filled out, muscles rippling underneath his sleek winter fur coat. Some might think he looked odd, with mismatched parts. Hunter's left ear flopped down while his right stood halfway up before folding down. He had a big blocky head but a long muzzle and his legs seemed a bit tall for his stout body. But to Will, Hunter was just perfect and walking in the bright sun bouncing off of the gleaming snow while the dog pranced about, the boy thought he must be about the luckiest that a person could be.

Scattered throughout and crisscrossing the trail to the clear cut, Will could every so often see the tracks of various critters that had already been exploring. He watched Hunter, nose to the ground, tearing off up the hill, and noticed the telltale groupings of four paw prints that showed a rabbit had hopped its way in that direction. Will could finally see what Hunter's nose always told him and was able to tell what the dog was chasing. "Wow, no wonder you are always so busy running off, Hunter! There are all kinds of creatures to chase, aren't there?"

Deer tracks, deep holes pounded by small hooves, were everywhere and were met with excitement every time Hunter came across them. More puzzling to Will were broad deep holes left by some bigger creature, that were spaced out by a large stride length but had been filled in somewhat by the snow that continued to fall. Perhaps a large wild cat or coyote; Will could not tell. But Hunter sure paid them cautious attention, stopping with his nose in the air and sniffing deeply and slowly as he sussed out what had been by. Will would have loved to know what predator left those but would have to rely on Hunter to tell whether there was any current threat.

After a morning exploring the hillside, Will was ready for a hot lunch. He joined his parents for left-over beef stew together with slices of warm bread fresh from the oven. Butter seeped into the fluffy sweet sponge of the bread that Will dredged in the stew gravy, and he was on his second piece before he noticed that Hunter had a long strand of drool hanging down from his jowls. "Well, someone else also worked up an appetite, didn't they boy?" He wasn't supposed to feed Hunter at the table, but Emma gave him a nod and Will shared a good-sized hunk of the gloppy goodness with the dog.

Chapter 16

The snow continued to fall all weekend. By Sunday there was a good foot on the ground around the cabin, and a good deal more up in the surrounding hills. Morning chores for Will included shoveling paths between the cabin and the woodshed, while Dan plowed their driveway with the tractor and Emma shoveled off their front and back porches.

They were all famished by lunch and wolfed deep red bowls of chili, brimming with all sorts of vegetables, beans, and beef, topped with bright yellow grated cheese and accompanied with crusty sourdough slices, toasted on the woodstove, that were dripping with luscious olive oil infused with minced garlic. His parents decided that a nap on the floor in front of the blazing woodstove was required, while Will decided that it was time to do some more playing in the snow.

Will strapped back on his snowshoes and took off with Hunter to see what other game signs they could find. They soon climbed their way up to the logging road in the clear cut above the house. Although they were looking for paw prints, what they found were tire treads. Hunter sniffed these deeply. "What are you finding, boy?" asked Will. "Looks like a truck came through to do some four-wheeling in the snow. I guess you can smell everywhere they have been, can't you?"

While Will liked to think of the woods above the cabin as his and Hunter's, they were connected by private logging roads to a network of primitive forest service roads, and others sometimes came to play. That was certainly the case when it snowed, as it seemed everyone with a shiny four-wheel-drive vehicle wanted to come find out what they could do. It wasn't unusual for urban drivers to find out their limits the hard way. Luckily the woods also tended to be patrolled by local young men, usually driving beat-up old pick-ups, on their way to and from unofficial shooting ranges in that National Forest. And the good-hearted locals were always happy to use their strong-running beaters to winch those shiny new imported SUVs and trucks out of whatever predicament they found themselves in. They felt good to be reminded that gobs of money did not make up for hard-earned practical knowledge and skill, and the rescued urbanites benefitted from having their manly self-esteem being taken down a notch or two.

Will and Hunter followed the tire tracks up the road, with Hunter chasing little finches that flitted around the snow-laden trees. But after a bit, Will noticed that the tracks stopped and reversed themselves – right off the roadbed and into a ravine! Peering downslope, Will could make out the back end of a black Nissan Frontier pickup, its red tail lights standing out in the falling snow. "Holy

Cow, Hunter, look at that truck! It will be hard to pull that one out. It's a good twenty feet down that ravine. Let's go check it out!"

The two made their way down the slope, Will bracing his feet in the broad snowshoes and Hunter descending in leaps. They soon reached the small truck but were puzzled to find it empty. Will felt the hood and found it to be cold to the touch. "This truck has been here all night, boy. The driver must have hiked out." Will wanted to be sure though, so he called loudly "Hello! Is anyone out there? Do you need help?"

Will called repeatedly and listened quietly each time, but heard no response. "OK boy, I guess they made it out. Let's keep on going." Will turned and started trudging back up the hill, but Hunter did not follow. Instead, he took off further down the slope, nose to the ground, zig-zagging along. "Oh, come on, Hunter. We'll be here all day – let's go!"

But Hunter persisted, going deeper and deeper down the ravine, until he came to a tall fir tree surrounded by a drift of snow, with a well in the snow surrounding the trunk. Here Hunter stopped and started digging, pausing after a bit to turn and bark towards Will and then returning to digging furiously.

Will had never seen Hunter act this way so he thought it best to see what had his dog so wound up. He trudged his way downhill and peered into the tree well. He was surprised to see something bright red. Will laid himself down flat – he knew from being in the high alpine woods with his parents that you had to be careful not to fall into a tree well – and started clearing away snow with his arms. The red item soon materialized to be a jacket!

Realizing the truck's driver had not made it out safely, Will kept moving away snow, aided by Hunter who continued to dig. Soon they uncovered the top half of a man, face covered by a neatly trimmed beard, wearing a black watch cap and with his arms crossed over his chest. Will shook the man "Hey Mister, are you OK?" The man did not respond, and his face was so pale. But Will persisted, and soon, had more of the man uncovered, surprised to see he had only jeans on his legs and fancy Timberland boots. Will then tried to pull the man out of the hole. He grabbed under each arm and tugged as hard as he could. He made no progress on moving him – but the man let out a groan as Will pulled on him. He was alive!

"Hunter, we need help! Would you stay here while I go get it? Stay! Do you understand?"

The dog seemed to understand and climbed in next to the man, curling up into a ball alongside the man, pressed hard against and laying partially on his torso.

"Good boy Hunter! I will be right back!"

Will climbed back up the hill and then tore down the road in as fast a waddling run as his snowshoes permitted. It only took him 30 minutes to get back home, but it felt like forever. He burst into the cabin. "Mom! Dad! Come quick – I found a man stuck in the snow up on the logging roads. He's really, really cold! We need to help him."

Emma immediately reached for her phone and called 911, where the dispatcher took all of the necessary information. She hung up and told Will that a search and recovery team from Olympic Mountain Rescue was being dispatched and would meet them at the cabin.

Within another thirty minutes, an ambulance pulled up that was towing a trailer on which two red snowmobiles were mounted. While one of the rescuers, a tall and very fit-looking man, unloaded the snowmobiles, the other, a petite but tough-looking woman, asked Will to tell them exactly where he had found the man. Will tried to explain but was having trouble making himself understood.

"Is it OK if your son goes with us, Ma'am?" asked the rescuer.

"Of course," answered Emma. "He knows the woods and roads around here better than most adults." Will climbed on one snowmobile behind the woman rescuer, while the male rescuer jumped on the other snowmobile to which was tied a plastic toboggan.

With Will's guidance, it did not take them long to find the truck that had fallen off the road. Will was relieved to see that Hunter was still with the man they had come to rescue.

"Stay here," said the male rescuer to Will. "We don't want you falling too."

Will was chastened – he had already been down and back, though he had his snowshoes that time. But he stayed put as the two rescuers made their way downhill after first tying a rope to the back of one of the snowmobiles. They tied the other end of the rope to the toboggan and slid it downhill with them. They worked down to the unconscious man and were greeted by Hunter. The dog wagged his tail at them but refused to move. It seemed that his body heat had done the man some good, as he was now groggily awake and moaning. "Ok boy, you did a good job. We'll take it from here."

But still, Hunter refused to move. "Hey, can you get your dog to back off?" hollered the male rescuer up to Will.

Will shouted back down "Good boy Hunter! Come!" And with that release, Hunter moved off the man and climbed back up to Will. The rescuers then pulled the cold man all of the way out of the snow and loaded him onto a blanket in the toboggan, which Will thought looked a lot like the plastic sled he had but that was a bit deeper and stiffer. Straps then were secured around the man from side to side in the toboggan. One across his chest, another across his hips, and the last round his lower legs.

The male rescuer then climbed up the hill and used a winch on one of the snowmobiles to pull the toboggan up with the rope while the woman guided it along the way. Soon they were all on their way back to the cabin.

As the rescuers loaded the recovered man into the back of the ambulance, the woman turned to Will and Emma. "Your son did a really fine thing here, Ma'am. And that dog – he probably saved this victim's life by warming him back up."

"Will he be OK?" asked Will.

"He is pretty hypothermic but, thanks to you and your dog, I think we made it in time. Thanks again."

And off they went. Will had such a sense of satisfaction from knowing that they had helped someone out. He wondered what it would take to become a mountain rescuer. But first – dinner! He was so hungry! And based on the way Hunter danced around the door into the kitchen, he guessed he was not alone.

"Come on boys, let's feed you. You surely earned a good dinner tonight!"

Chapter 17

"Do your part – Help us fined wild dogs! Reward - $250.

Text the CERT Agency at 800-DOG-FIND."

Dan and Will looked at the flyer posted on the bulletin board at the Cenex feed store with trepidation. Dan knew that any natural dog turned into the CERT Agency would be eliminated. Just like they were vermin. Dan subconsciously wrapped a gentle hand about Hunter's withers and looked around nervously, suddenly wondering if there was anyone in town cruel and suspicious enough to send a tip in about the dog's somewhat unusual origin story. Will looked up at his father. "Why do they want to pay people for wild dogs, Dad? What will they do with them?" Dan straightened his spine, put on an air of false confidence, and said "Don't worry Will, we have Hunter covered, nothing is going to happen to him."

Will took comfort from his father's answer and did not press further. But a little worm of worry had taken hold and twisted somewhere deep in his gut. Will vowed to himself that he would do whatever he needed to do to protect his dog and best friend. "We're going to go meet Ryan and Hank at the ball field, Dad. I will be back home before dinner."

Dan lifted Will's bicycle out of the truck and took one more look around. "Alright Will. And, just in case, keep Hunter close by you, OK?"

Will pedaled onto the ball field, Hunter loping alongside. They were a little early for the meet-up, and Will busied himself rolling large snowballs for building a snowman out of the last of the melting white stuff that covered parts of the field. Hunter in the meantime was on the scent of a mouse burrowed deep in the grass, zig-zagging back and forth with his nose crammed in the grass.

Soon Ryan showed up, riding his bike. He rode with one arm stretched out, trailing Hank on a leash. "Don't you ever worry that Hank will get tangled up in your spokes?" asked Will.

"Not really. This is just so he doesn't wander off and get hit by a car or go see another dog." Will thought it worked for Ryan and Hank, but he could never see putting Hunter on a leash. His dog stayed with Will because he wanted to, not because he had to do so. The freedom that Hunter had in choosing to stay with Will is what made his friendship so valuable.

While the boys were talking, Hunter pounced on the mouse he had been hunting. He flipped it up in the air, then caught it again. It did not look like much fun for the mouse, though at least Hunter did not eat it because of all the food that he was being fed by Will's family. Will did not want to see the mouse suffer. "Come on boy, let's go!" Hunter broke off from the mouse, which scurried back under some tall grass.

The boys and their dogs started to ride back into town, Hank still on his leash and Hunter exploring with nose to ground while they went on.

Just then a large truck glided by, driven by a pair of CERT agents. The truck pulled up alongside the boys. The older of the two agents, sitting in the passenger seat, put down his window. He was a gnarled man, with a face as craggy as the surface of the moon, pitted by craters. The badge on his chest pocket said "DEVUS". "Have you boys seen any wild dogs around here? We had a report that there was one in town."

"No sir, we have not," answered Will. "That's right," Ryan agreed. The agent frowned and looked briefly at Hank and then at Hunter. He paused and turned his focus back to Hunter. The agent next to Officer Devus, who Will recognized as Agent Rudy, leaned across the seat of the truck and whispered to his older partner. "That sure is an odd-looking dog you have there," said Officer Devus. "Where did you get it?"

"It's a clone of my grandparents' dog."

"Hmmm, well, if you say so," replied Officer Devus, scratching his bristly jowl suspiciously. "But keep an eye out for wild dogs, will you? Those fleabags often carry diseases, including rabies. Why there was even a rabid dog that stole a baby the next county over. So, you'll tell us if you find a wild dog masquerading as a Gen dog, won't you? Or even as a clone, right? You wouldn't want a little kid being hurt on your conscience, would you?"

Will gulped and put a hand on Hunter protectively. "No sir. I mean yes sir, I will. I mean I don't know of any but will tell you if I do."

"OK then. We'll be keeping an eye out, including on you, young man." With that, the agent put the window back up and rode slowly up. As he passed, Will could see a mottled-colored dog laying in the bed of the truck. It was limp and flopped like a wet noodle as the truck drove over a speed bump. With a sickening feeling, Will began to suspect what happened to wild dogs that were caught.

Hunter smelled the air as the truck continued, let out a whine, and looked up at Will with big brown eyes. "Come on boy, it's OK. But we better head home now."

The boys and dogs started back to their homes. "Are you OK, Will?" asked Ryan. "You don't look so good." Will's entire body was shaking as he rode along, and he was fighting tears.

"Did you see that dead dog in the back of the truck?" stammered Will. "Why would they do that?"

"Yea, that is too bad," replied Ryan. "But at least it was just a wild dog."

Will screeched his bike to a stop. "At least? At least? Why should that matter?" Will was angry now, and the anger settled his nerves. "Someone might have loved that dog."

"OK, calm down. I am sorry, I did not mean to upset you. But really, no one would have cared about a wild dog." As Ryan was speaking, Hunter laid his head against Will's thigh, pressing in to comfort the distressed boy. Will unconsciously rubbed Hunter's head and ears as he steadied himself.

All of a sudden, the light went on for Ryan. "Wait, is Hunter a clone?"

Will did not answer, but put an arm protectively around Hunter's neck and glared at his friend.

"Holy cow, don't answer that," said Ryan as he looked around nervously. "Do you know how much trouble you could get into? Why if anyone found out that Hunter is a…"

"Shut up!" whispered Will loudly. "You can't tell anyone. Hunter is a good dog! He hasn't done anything to hurt anyone! And either have I."

"Oh man, Will. I always thought it was a little funny how you ended up with a dog all of a sudden. But of course, I won't say anything. You are my best bud, Will. I would never do anything to hurt you."

Relaxing his shoulders, Will let out a long exhale. "Thanks, Ryan. You don't know what this pup means to me. But remember, nobody can find out."

With that, the boys continued to their homes.

Chapter 18

Spring was working its magic, and it seemed everything around Will's cabin was green. Not just green, but electric green, with so many different shades of vivid lushness. The fir trees had deep forest green interiors capped with bright lime-green new growth on the ends of their branches. The big leaf maple leaves were spreading out like giant emerald fans. Cottonwoods, alder, cherry, all competed with different green hues, from the dark green of new grass shoots to the light hue of a lacewing fly, that pulsed vibrantly with life. Sometimes, like today, Will took the time to look and was amazed at how much new energy surrounded him, all of nature exclaiming that it was time for renewal.

Will thought how lucky he was to live in an area that was naturally so rich and verdant, knowing that on the other side of the Cascade Mountains in the Eastern side of the state people walked around in dust relieved only by deep water irrigation. He had heard his parents wonder how long those aquifers could last, as people frittered that resource away to make what ought to have been a desert bear fruit.

His musings were interrupted by a deep thrumming that seemed to be growing closer and louder. Soon a helicopter flew overhead, virtually on top of them, causing Hunter, who had been sleeping sprawled out on cool grass, to sit up and shrink against Will. As the helicopter passed and climbed up towards the clear cuts above their cabin, the machine banked and Will observed a man looking out through binoculars with a rifle perched on his lap, the barrel of which stuck out the open cockpit door. The CERT logo was emblazoned on the tail of the chopper.

Dan came out from the barn, looking up with his eyes shielded as the helicopter passed out of view, and in the distance, in either direction, they could hear two other choppers heading in the same direction. The combined vibration of these big metal birds seemed to shake the whole house, and soon Emma also joined them from the chicken coop. "It looks like that rumored round-up is happening," said Emma quietly to Dan.

Just then a truck, also bearing the red and black CERT logo, pulled into the yard. An agent leaned out his window, lifted his sunglasses, and directed his attention to Dan and Emma. "We had a report that there are wild dogs up in the hills around your place. Have you folks seen or heard anything?"

While Dan and Emma were shaking their heads, Will drew in a sharp breath, recognizing Agent Devus from their encounter in town over the winter. Putting his hand on Hunter's head, he silently urged the dog behind him.

"How about you, boy, have you seen any signs of mongrels about?"

"Oh, uh, no sir, I sure have not."

"Say, I remember you. You had that goofy-looking clone dog, didn't you? Is that him?"

"Oh, yes sir. This is Hunter."

"I have never seen a clone or a GenDog for that matter, that looks like him. You sure about him being a clone?"

"He sure is, Officer," broke in Dan, putting an arm protectively around Will. "Now, if that is all you needed, we'll get back to work."

The agent stared at Dan for a moment, then nodded and put his truck in gear, and started to drive off slowly. Will could see him looking back in the review mirror at Hunter while holding a radio mic in his hand into which he spoke.

All afternoon, Will, Dan, and Emma heard the sound of helicopters overhead and trucks revving up in the hills surrounding their cabin. Occasionally the report of a rifle echoed through the valley. Finally, at about dusk, the CERT team called it a day. Emma had gone down in a utility vehicle to gather the day's mail at a mailbox at the bottom of the hill. When riding the UTV back up their road to home, she passed a group of trucks driving downhill. She pulled over into the ditch to let them pass, and could not help but see a limp pile of dogs, blood staining different colors of fur, in the bed of one of them. Emma put her head into her hands and wept. After a time, she regained her composure and headed back to the cabin to share the grim news.

It was a sad night for her family, wondering whether any of Hunter's relatives might have been in that pile. It pained them all to think of creatures, so formerly full of life, having been reduced to inanimate waste. How could people be so cruel? Will hugged Hunter extra close in bed that night, the dog's fur absorbing tears that continued to seep until he fell asleep.

Chapter 19

It had been a quiet summer, and Will was enjoying hiking with Hunter to a small lake nestled at the base of a ravine between the foothills. He cast a length of fishing line into the water, using a maple sapling as a rod. A small weight was secured on the end of the line, and then a hook baited with a grasshopper. He pulled in the line and then sent it out again, over and over.

Suddenly the line started to go deeper into the water, and Will pulled it back to find a small trout, no more than six inches long, flopping on the end. The tiny fish was gorgeous, yellow with black specks and a red stripe down its side. He flipped it up onto the rocky beach to take out the barbless hook, intending to place it gently back into the water. But Hunter spied the flopping fish, which slipped off the hook and just as quickly was scooped up by the dog. "Hunter, NO!" yelled Will, just as the fish disappeared down the dog's throat. Hunter sat down with a puzzled look, stunned by the rare rebuke. "That one was too little!" The dog crawled over to Will and pressed his head into the boy's lap, looking for forgiveness. Will thought he really could not blame the dog for eating when a meal presented itself, after all, it was how he had survived on his own before being taken in by the boy's family. "Just sit back next time Hunter, OK? Little fish need to be given a chance to grow up into big ones." Will stroked Hunter's head and could not possibly stay mad at him.

The two continued fishing for a while longer but did not catch anything else. "Let's go home and get some dinner boy. You may have had a snack already, you little bugger, but I am still hungry."

Walking back towards home, Hunter darted off into the woods down a game trail and was pawing at something in the brush. The dog was so engrossed in whatever it had found that it ignored Will's persistent calls. Will took a look at the sky, which was growing dusky. "Come on Hunter, we have to go." But still, the dog ignored him, which was unusual. Will made his way through the gap in the trees and brush to Hunter.

"What do you have there that is so good boy?" Will could see Hunter pawing at something reddish brown that was covered by a layer of loose branches and leaves. Moving away the debris, Will spotted a hoof on the end of a narrow leg that extended up to a bloodied cavity and realized he was looking at the carcass of a deer. Involuntarily shuddering, Will stood and looked around, nervously glancing over each shoulder and then looking up in the overhead boughs of the surrounding trees. "Come on Hunter, leave it. We have to go now." He knew exactly what he was looking at, as there was only one predator in these parts of the woods that was both large enough to take down a deer and that covered its kill. He also knew that a cougar whose kill had been disturbed could be dangerously protective.

Tapping his hand on his thigh, he again told Hunter to "leave it" and started back to the logging road. Sensing the tension in Will's voice, this time Hunter listened and left the fascinating deer stash to follow Will. Just as the two were almost to the road, Hunter suddenly stopped and started to whine, moving to stand in front of Will. The fur on the dog's back stood straight up, which made the hair on the back of Will's neck do the same.

"What is wrong, boy? Come on, I don't like being out here this late, especially with a fresh kill so close." Will attempted to push by Hunter, but the dog stood firmly in place and let out a whine. Will noticed that Hunter was staring intently ahead of them. Will looked down the trail towards the light of the clearing around the road and saw what he most feared. A large heavily muscled tawny cat crouched low, with yellow eyes staring hard at Will, and the tip of its tail twitching back and forth.

Will had never been so scared in all of his life. His parents had taught him from his earliest days what to do if he encountered a cougar, which roamed the Olympic National Park and National Forest but also freely prowled the woods surrounding the cabin. He had never actually seen a mountain lion, as cougars were also known. The elusive cats generally steered clear of humans. But they would protect a meal, and Will knew he had to be very careful.

Will recalled that he needed to maintain eye contact with the cougar because if he looked away the cat, which was an ambush predator, might pounce. He needed to look and sound big, to appear as un-deer-like as possible, making it clear that he was not the big cat's favorite prey. He should back slowly away from the cat, but never run, which triggered the cat's chase instinct. As a last resort, if attacked, he needed to fight back, hard. Unlike with a bear, he had been taught, "playing dead" would get you eaten.

Will stared the powerful cat in the eyes, willing himself not to blink. Holding Hunter's collar with one hand, he waved his other arm and flapped his jacket, yelling loudly "Get! Go away!" But the cougar stayed in place and even took a stealthy step forward, all the while staring intently at the boy, waiting for him to make a mistake. The cat was so locked onto Will that it did not even seem to notice Hunter. Will was in such a dilemma – going forward took him closer to the cougar, but backing away would take him straight back to the deer cached in the brush, which is what the cat was protecting. He was stuck and thought feverishly about what to do. In his peripheral vision, Will spotted a stout tree limb. He remembered hearing of instances when people were able to chase off cougars with rocks or sticks. He started to bend to grab the stick when he remembered that you were not supposed to bend over in the presence of a mountain lion, as it diminished your size. It seemed he could not make the right move!

But something had to give, as the cat took yet another step closer, and Hunter began to growl. Will gripped

Hunter's collar more firmly and started to squat down to lower himself closer to the tree branch while keeping his torso upright and tall. Feeling for the limb, he found only ferns and instinctively glanced towards the branch for which he strived.

Looking away with that momentary glance was a mistake, and the cougar sprang for Will. It was an amazingly strong animal and launched itself to clear the twenty-five feet between it and Will in a single leap. Just as Will realized his mistake, he was pulled off his feet by Hunter, who leaped up in the air to intercept the flying cat. The cougar would have landed on Will's head to grab his neck in powerful jaws, but instead, it was met by a growling and snapping dog. Hunter hit the cougar in the chest, deflecting the cat and its sharp fangs from his boy.

In the process, the cat raked Hunter's side with its claws, slicing through the dog's fur and spilling blood from a striped set of lacerations as the dog and big cat were both knocked aside. Hunter ignored his wounds as he landed with a thud, rolled back to his feet, and started after the cougar again, snapping and snarling and worrying the cat about its face. At the same time, Will had found the tree limb and swung it wildly at the cat while making a guttural shout as loud as he could. The cougar finally realized that he was not dealing with prey, and turned and ran off. Hunter continued the chase a few yards, but then faltered and sunk to the ground.

Will, though dazed and afraid the cat might return, went immediately to Hunter. "You saved me, old buddy. Oh, but you are hurt so bad! Hold on Hunter, I will get you home." Using strength that he did not know he had, Will picked up Hunter and hugged him close to his chest. He made it down the game trail to the logging road, glancing back every few steps and relieved to see that the cougar did not seem to have returned.

Will slowly walked back home, staggering under his load, and stopping frequently to rest and look behind and around him. He kept waiting for the cougar to return and was terrified that it would pounce on them from behind. It grew darker and darker and what was often a 15-minute walk soon turned into an hour and they still had a good way to go. Will did not think he could make it all the way carrying Hunter, but there was no way he would leave his friend behind. For the second time that night, Will did not know what to do.

But then in the distance, Will heard his parents calling him and saw flashlights bobbing along down the road. "Mom! Dad! Over here! Come quick – Hunter's hurt bad!"

Chapter 20

Dan, Emma, and Will rushed into the receiving area of the emergency veterinary clinic in the neighboring town, carrying Hunter in a large fleece blanket that they used as a makeshift stretcher. Hunter had lost a lot of blood by the time they were able to get him home, loaded into the truck, and to the clinic. Will was trying hard not to remember the feel of the thick warm blood that had seeped through the blanket onto his lap, draining his precious dog's energy.

They had called ahead to warn Dr. McKay that they were coming in. The vet met them at the door and made a sad but determined face when she saw Hunter. "Will he be OK?" asked Will?

"I promise I will do all I can to save your dog, Will," said Dr. McKay. Although she worked at the emergency clinic during off-hours one night a week, she knew Will's family from her regular practice. She knew how much Hunter meant to Will but wanted to make sure she did not promise more than she could deliver.

As Dr. McKay and a vet tech carried Hunter into a surgery room, the dog looked pleadingly at Will and whimpered, somehow finding the energy to thump his tail once. "Please, can I go back with him?" asked Will.

"I am sorry Will, but we are full up with several emergency injuries to deal with. Things are too busy and it would not be safe for you. We'll let you know as soon as we have a better idea of what is going on with Hunter."

Emma put an arm around Will as he sadly watched Hunter leave. "See you soon Boy. You'll be OK. We'll be right here waiting for you."

It was a surprisingly busy night and the clinic was full of people waiting anxiously for their pets. Will sat on a plastic-upholstered couch, Emma on one side and Dan on the other, each with an arm around him to lend comfort. To distract himself, he watched people and animals come and go and wondered what their stories were.

A young couple, at least somewhat younger than Will's parents, came in walking a large German Shephard dog. At least they attempted to walk the dog. Its hind legs were withered away, and they supported the dog's back half with a sling under its belly. The Shephard's coat was mottled with grey, and its eyes were slightly fogged over. It was clear that the dog had had a good life but was nearing its end. Collapsing onto the floor, the dog nonetheless pressed its muzzle onto the woman's lap and thumped its large, arthritic tail. The woman stroked the dog's head and gazed into his eyes, whispering.

"How old is your dog?" asked Will. The woman looked up and gave Will a kindly smile. "He is 14 years old," she answered.

"What is wrong with him?" continued Will.

The woman looked lovingly at her dog with tears in her eyes. "I think he just ran out of energy. He cannot make it up on four legs anymore."

"Can Dr. McKay make your dog better?" Will asked again.

"That's enough Will," broke in Emma. "I am sorry," said Emma to the woman. "I just don't think Will has ever seen an old dog before."

"Well, there are not many of those anymore, are there?" answered the woman. "Old Rocky here is our last. He is a clone of the first dog we had after we married. We sure miss that dog, and we will miss Rocky too."

The woman's husband broke in then and said that the Vet tech was ready for them. The couple eased Rocky up and half-carried him with the sling into a back room, the door closing behind them.

"How come they got to go back with their dog and we did not?" Will asked Emma.

"I think they are going to say goodbye to Rocky," answered Emma. "They are in a peaceful room, not like the emergency surgery that Hunter is in."

Half an hour later, the couple came out. Alone. It was evident that both had been crying. They thanked the receptionist and went slowly from the clinic to their car.

Two hours later, Dr. McKay came out and walked over to Will and his parents. She looked tired but was smiling. Will felt immediately relieved to see that look.

"Looks like your dog is going to be OK, folks," said Dr. McKay. "He was very weak, but it is clear that he is a fighter and wants to get back to you. And luckily no major arteries were torn. It took 56 stitches and three units of blood, but I am pleased to tell you that Hunter should make a full recovery."

"Thank you! Thank you!" chorused the whole family. "Can we take him home now?" asked Dan.

"We need to keep Hunter overnight just to keep an eye on him. Assuming he does OK overnight, which he should, you can pick him up at my office tomorrow morning."

Chapter 21

The whole family seemed to rush through breakfast the next morning, then waited impatiently until 9:00 when Dr. McKay's office would be open. They went to her office and were the first ones in the door, taking a seat to wait for their dog.

While waiting, a middle-aged woman came in walking a beautiful brindle-colored boxer. The dog had a brilliant white chest and forelegs and white across her snout, which offset the black and reddish banded striping of her coat. The dog glowed with youth and vitality, with clear eyes and floppy ears. She was almost hopping on her leash with excitement and stuck her stubby muzzle into every nook and cranny to smell whatever secret scents were there. Bouncing over to Will, she smelled and licked his hands while Will rubbed her ears.

"Wow, your dog is a beauty! And what a sweet puppy she is!" exclaimed Will.

"Well, she is not a puppy," said the woman. "She will be ten years old tomorrow. We are just here for her annual booster shots."

"I would have never guessed ten," said Emma. "I would have guessed she was no more than one."

"Our Sadie-girl is our third boxer, but our first GenDog. None of our others made it to ten. They had tumors and other problems. But they sure fixed that with our Sadie! I just hope I can keep up with her energy!" laughed the woman.

Just then an exam room door opened, and a vet tech called back Will's family. They had only a few moments to wait further, and then Dr. McKay walked in with Hunter. The dog was walking on his own, though stiffly and somewhat gingerly, and one side of his fur was shaved bare. The bristly stubble was crisscrossed by lines of black stitches, looking like ants on a log. But as soon as Hunter saw them, his whole body erupted into a wiggle and his tail thumped the door frame so hard it sounded like he would crack the wood.

"Oh buddy, it's so good to see you!" exclaimed Will as he leaned down to hug Hunter. He could not help but start crying, so great was his joy and relief at having his precious friend back. Emma and Dan each also misted up and thanked the vet profusely for having saved Hunter.

"Well, it's only right that we could save Hunter after he so bravely saved Will," said Dr. McKay. "You sure have yourself one good dog there, don't you Will?"

Will simply nodded and continued to hug Hunter as the dog gave the boy sloppy kisses, wiping his tears away with a wet tongue.

"You'll need to keep Hunter's stitches dry and come back at the end of next week to have them removed," said Dr. McKay.

"No problem at all," said Dan. "And again, we are so appreciative for all that you did for Hunter."

"There is one delicate matter we do need to discuss," continued the vet. "Looking at the wear on Hunter's teeth and his gum line, it is evident that Hunter is a normal, healthy two-year-old dog."

"Why yes, he is about two, what about it?" asked Emma.

"What I mean is he is a normal two-year-old. We are just starting to see the very first signs of a tiny bit of aging. So, he is not a GenDog, is he?"

"Oh, no. See, he is a clone of my Mother's dog," said Dan.

"But the thing is, I looked for Hunter in the clone registry, and I did not find him," continued Dr. McKay. "I did not find any clones registered to your family."

Dan looked down for a few moments, and then looked up sadly at the veterinarian. Will, following the conversation, looked nervously back and forth between his mother and father. This could not be happening, he thought.

Dan started to speak when Dr. McKay held up her hand. "Just stop there, Dan. Please don't tell me anything I should not hear. You may not be aware that veterinarians have mandatory reporting requirements when they discover natural dogs."

"But…" started Emma.

"Hold on, let me finish," said Dr. McKay. "Now of course I am going to have to follow the law, even if I think it is stupid and unconscionable. But as I read the law, I don't have to report anything I don't know for 100% certainty."

At this Dan and Emma clammed right up and smiled and nodded with appreciation. Will still was not sure exactly what was going on, but he could tell from the relieved looks on his parents' faces that things were going to be OK.

"I just wanted to warn you, to make sure it is me personally that you see to take Hunter's stitches out and to be careful overall. Not everyone thinks the same that I do. And Hunter is such a good boy. So, just be very careful, OK?"

The family again thanked Dr. McKay and gratefully drove Hunter home.

Sitting in his bed that night, Will stroked Hunter's head as the dog snuggled close. It had been a wild couple of days. He thought how vulnerable life had proven to be. And while he was so, so happy to have Hunter back, he also realized that he would not have him forever. Even as young as Hunter was, he now realized that Hunter's life would be far shorter than he would wish. And just as Will slowly rationed his favorite Christmas candies to make them last, really tasting and slowly eating each piece, the measured time he would have with Hunter made it all the sweeter. He vowed to savor every moment.

Chapter 22

In all of his twelve years, Will had rarely been so determined. He pedaled furiously uphill as he made his way home. Hunter, long recovered from his wounds, faint scaring barely visible under his fur, loped along beside Will, muscular and in the prime of his life. It was early summer and the green grasses that lined the road were just beginning to show shades of copper and wheat as they started to dry out from the warm air.

Running into the cabin, he shouted "Mom, I have a job! Ryan is helping the Valley Farm buck and stack hay bales, and they need another hand. It's just for a couple of weeks now and a couple of more weeks at the end of the summer. That would be OK, right?"

"Bucking hay bales is a lot of work, Will. Bales of local grass hay run 50-60 pounds each. Do you think you can handle that all day?" answered Emma.

"Sure, I can do that, I am pretty strong for my age. And I could save up money for a car."

"A car, huh? Aren't you getting ahead of yourself? Sixteen is a long way away." Emma stood back and looked at her boy, and had to admit that he was starting to look like a teenager. He had sprouted up to already stand taller than her, though not as tall as Dan, and was starting to fill out. All the running, biking, and motorbiking up and down the hills had helped him grow strong. But she was not quite ready to say goodbye to having a young child around.

"I know if I want a car someday, I will have to pay for it. And I can start driving with you on a permit when I am 15. So that is just three years away. I imagine it will take me a while to save up enough. This would be a start. Ryan is not strong enough to handle all of the work, and we can do it together and split the pay. And the farm manager says I can take Hunter with me. Ryan takes Hank along, and they seem to have a good time. Can I Mom, please?"

Emma could not think of a way to argue against this mature logic, and so she agreed.

Will rode his bike up the rural highway to the Valley Farm early the next morning, as Hunter loped along with excitement, wondering where they could be going at first light. They met Ryan at the farm as he and Hank were being dropped off.

Farmer Joe met them and explained to Will how things worked. The hay fields had been cut the last week and farmer Joe was getting ready to drive over the field in successive passes on a newer green John Deer tractor that pulled a red hay baler. The baler scooped up the cut hay, compacted it into large rectangular bricks, wrapped twine around each, and spit out perfect hay bales that each was secured with two bands of twine.

Will and Ryan's jobs were to follow the baler. One would drive the old blue Ford tractor that pulled a flatbed trailer, and the other would follow on foot, grabbing the hay bales by the twine and swinging the bales up onto the trailer. They would take turns driving and bucking the hay bales. Both had learned earlier on the tree farm run by Will's parents how to drive a tractor, which was a simple matter of stopping and starting with the tractor stuck in gear and the throttle level stuck at the desired speed, and without the need to operate a clutch.

They started with Will driving the old Ford tractor forward in the lowest gear possible, and Ryan bucking the bales. After half an hour Ryan was exhausted, taking longer and longer to get each bale onto the trailer. At first, he could jerk a bale clean off the ground and onto the trailer. But at the end of the first row, he would have to lift just one end of the bale and rest it against the trailer and then flip the other end up. Farmer Joe came by at this point, going the opposite direction in the adjoining row with the baler, and suggested they switch.

As much as Will had enjoyed driving the tractor, he was eager to show off his strength bucking the hay bales. He found he could easily lift the sixty-pound bales onto the trailer in one smooth jerk. He loved the dry grassy smell of the hay, which somehow made him think both of rolling down fresh green summer hills and of jumping into dry piles of autumn leaves. While Hank had dozed in the sun as Ryan worked, Hunter ran along looking for field mice that occasionally scurried out of hiding as they were disturbed by the nearby baler. Hunter would listen and then pounce in the hay stubble to catch each one, snapping and tossing the poor creatures into the air. He still had excellent hunting skills but would break off and leave them go, rather than eat them when told to "leave it" by Will.

Will managed to keep up longer than Ryan, going strong for the full half-hour, but then he too started to flag. After 45 minutes it was clear that he was struggling, as it seemed he was having more and more difficulty moving the hay bales. It was time to switch, and they did so as directed by Farmer Joe.

The two continued this way all day, taking occasional breaks to snack on cookies that Emma had made for the boys and frosty thermoses of lemonade that Ryan had bought along. By two o'clock in the afternoon, as the day's heat grew, it was time to call it quits. Both boys were tired, dusty, and sweaty. But this was forgotten when Farmer Joe called them over and gave each $50 cash for their troubles for the day. The farmer peeled one and five dollar bills off of a wad from the front pocket of his overalls so that each boy ended up with a thick stack of bills that almost did not fit in their jeans' pockets. It was a huge sum of money for either boy but meant a lot to Will, whose family always lived so close to the edge.

"I am going to use this money to buy a new RC truck," said Ryan as they walked to the parking area to wait for rides home, referring to the Remote-Control toy vehicles that the boys enjoyed racing. "What about you?"

"I am saving up so I can get a real car when I am old enough," answered Will.

"Really? That's so far away! Why not enjoy it now?" responded Ryan. "I figure my folks will buy me a car when I turn 16. They did for my sister. I just have to keep my grades up."

Will couldn't fathom how easy some things came to Ryan, whose family had so many more resources. But he also wondered how many things that were not earned were valued by his friend. For instance, while Ryan enjoyed having Hank, he was all too quick to ditch his dog when inconvenient, like when going to the movie theatre. Not Will – he could not imagine missing out on a day with Hunter before he had to do so when school started back up.

Chapter 23

Ryan and Will worked their hay bale job on and off all summer, being called in whenever the hay was long enough to be cut and baled. They labored furiously during baling of the first cutting at the beginning of the summer, and again mid-summer after the second cutting, and finally for the third and final cutting of the summer. The hay tended to be dryer and not as lush at the end of the summer but still made decent fodder. A plus for Will and Ryan is that the third-cutting hay bales were lighter; a minus is that the hay they baled, and the very air in which they labored, was laden with dust.

It was the next to last day, and the work was so dusty that Will found that when he blew his nose, more dirt came out than mucus. Snot dirtballs, his Dad called them. And his ears would likewise trap a lot of dust, leaving Q-tips dirty when Will cleaned his ears after a shower. But Will had managed to save up a good portion of his pay over the summer, most of which would go into his future-car fund. But he was excited to be able to use some to treat his parents to something special. Maybe his Dad could use some new work gloves and his Mom some really good quality olive oil and balsamic vinegar. Or maybe he would take them all out to their favorite Mexican restaurant for dinner one night. Thinking through the possibilities of how he might surprise his parents with something nice for a change, when they did so much for him every day, made him almost giddy in anticipation.

But first, he needed to finish this day and the next, and then he could decide what best to do. They were nearing the last row for the day, and Will was driving a tractor while Ryan bucked the bales. They had both grown much stronger over the summer and settled easily into a rhythm as they worked.

As the two went down the row, they spotted Hank laying sprawled out in the sunny, tall grass of the adjacent row. The dog would soon be in the way of Farmer Joe and his bailer, which was heading towards them in the opposite row. Will spied the situation and hollered at Hank to get out of the way. But the dog was out cold.

Will could not believe the dog was so oblivious and yelled again louder this time. While he still did not roust Hank, he caught Hunter's attention, who started barking in reaction to Will's excited voice. Hank raised a lazy head and looked at Will, but did not move. The situation was proving to be dangerous, as Farmer Joe was approaching Hank with the bailer. Luckily, the farmer spied the dog, and veered his tractor and baler to the right to go around the dog, just as Ryan sprang into action and headed at a sprint towards Hank.

Later Will had trouble explaining exactly what happened next because it happened so fast. Farmer Joe turned the tractor steering wheel right while looking behind and left to make sure he missed Hank with the baler at the same instant that Ryan sprang out towards his dog to move it.

Ryan reached down to grab Hank's collar, sticking his right leg out behind to balance as he leaned down on his left knee. Unfortunately, focused as he was on Hank, he missed seeing the baler swing wide behind Farmer Joe's tractor. The baler ran over Ryan's right leg and sliced through his tendon between his ankle and calf, cutting nearly to the bone. Ryan fell to the ground with a scream as his lower leg turned the freshly cut hay blood red. Things happened fast then. Ryan's scream was so loud that Farmer Joe heard it over the tractor, which he stalled and leaped down from at a run. Hank sat stunned, trying to figure out what had just happened as Ryan rolled on the ground in agony. Will cut the engine on his tractor and also hopped down, still unable to process what he was seeing, which was his friend bleeding profusely and clearly in pain.

Farmer Joe took off his shirt, ripped off a sleeve, and tied it tightly around Ryan's ankle to staunch the bleeding. He then loaded Ryan onto the hay bale trailer and told Will to drive slowly and carefully back to the barn. In the meantime, Farmer Joe took out his cell phone and called emergency medical services.

Will had no appetite for dinner that night, as he waited at home for an update on Ryan. Finally, at 9:00 that night, Ryan's father called. He talked to Emma for a few minutes, with Emma nodding and sounding relieved. When she finally hung up, she turned to Will and said "Ryan will be just fine. He was in surgery for three hours but his leg and tendons are all stitched back together. It will take a few months to heal and then therapy for a few more months, but he should come out the other side just fine and be able to run and walk like nothing ever happened. So, relax, Ryan will be OK."

"Oh man, that is just great! When can I go see him? Does he want me to exercise Hank?" asked Will.

"Well, there is a bit more news, son," said Emma. "Ryan's parents were understandably very upset that he was hurt, and they believe it happened because Hank was so zoned out that he would not get out of the way of the farm equipment. They think Hank is a safety risk for Ryan, and plan on turning Hank back into the GenDog exchange run by CERT."

"Oh wow, that is so not good. That will upset Ryan. It only happened once – why do they have to get rid of Hank?"

"It's hard for you to understand what a parent will do to protect their child, Will. I don't know, they may be over-reacting. But I can't judge without being in their shoes. Maybe there is something about GenDog's that makes them less alert."

Ryan thought of how oblivious Hank was to mice and squirrels. Maybe there was something to that. But to get rid of someone's dog? He could not imagine his parents ever doing that with Hunter.

"What will happen to Hank?" asked Will.

"CERT runs the GenDog Exchange to try to match up dogs whose owners died or cannot keep them with new owners," answered Emma. "They also try to find replacement GenDogs for owners whose GenDogs get hit by cars or such. Also, anybody can buy a "used" GenDog, though CERT won't place a GenDog unless the GenDog's engineered life span fairly well matches the expected life span of the new owner."

"Wow, it sounds like a used car service or something," said Will. "I cannot imagine anyone else ending up with Hunter, or me wanting a different dog than Hunter. You can't just swap out people and dogs, that is not right."

"It's funny you mention that, Will," answered Emma. "Ryan's Dad remembered you wanted a GenDog a couple of years ago, and he wanted to know if we wanted to buy Hank."

"What? Buy my friend's dog? That's weird. Plus, I already have Hunter, the best dog in the world."

Emma smiled at Will's assessment of Hunter. He was a patchwork mongrel, but she had to admit that she felt the same way. "I am sure he was just trying to help you out, Will. I told him thanks, but we were not interested."

"Mom, what happens if nobody wants to buy Hank from the GenDog Exchange?"

Emma exchanged a knowing look with Dan. "Don't worry about it, Will. I am sure something will work out for Hank." At least Emma sure hoped so, but she did not add that last thought out loud.

Chapter 24

Will did not see much more of Ryan that summer. But he was happy to hear that Ryan was returning to school and excited to see his friend the first day that he was able to return. As Will arrived at school on his bicycle, he saw Ryan's Dad pulling into the parking lot. Ryan soon hopped out, although "hop" was not quite the way to describe it. He sort of eased out of the front seat and then used the open-door frame to hoist himself out of the car.

"Ryan!" hollered Will. Upon seeing him, Ryan grinned ear to ear and started walking over to Will, waving at his Dad over the shoulder. Will walked with a bit of a limp now. It looked like all the physical therapy Will knew Ryan had been doing had helped him a good deal, but more would be needed before Ryan would be back to himself.

"Hey man, really good to see you!" said Ryan. Will patted his buddy on the back. "You too! Talking on the phone has been great and all, but it's just not the same. Want to hang out this afternoon?" The boys decided to get ice cream after school and then walk to the nearby marina to scout out the local and visiting boats.

"Ryan, I've got this," said Will as he handed a ten-dollar bill to the clerk at the ice cream shop. Will had saved up more money than he expected working solo with Farmer Joe at the very end of summer. He could not wait to try the tangerine ice cream with chocolate chips he had picked out, while Ryan went for huckleberry.

As they walked through town to the marina, they savored their ice cream and just being together again after a weird ending to the summer break. They were catching up when Hunter came tearing down the road towards them. "Whoa boy, what are you doing here?" Will said as he grabbed Hunter by the collar, though the dog was dancing in place and staring hard at Will's ice cream and hardly seemed at risk of running off.

"I guess when he did not see me get off the bus Hunter decided to find me," apologized Will. "I should scold him for coming into town on his own, but how can I be angry at that face?" Hunter was firmly in a sit but somehow still dancing from haunch to haunch, tail wagging madly, profusely offering a paw and giving Will a good case of puppy dog eyes. "Man, he is a good dog, isn't he?" said Will as he gave Hunter a taste of ice cream.

Will realized too late that he might have unintentionally hurt his friend's feelings. "Sorry Ryan, I wasn't thinking. I am so, so sorry that you had to get rid of Hank."

"It's OK Will, it was tough but I understand where my Dad was coming from" answered Ryan. "It's weird though, I was supposed to have Hank my whole life, and now he's gone. I thought having a GenDog meant that was something I would never have to face."

"Do you mind if I ask what happened to Hank?"

"I was afraid Hank would not find a new home. I made my Dad promise that he would be sure that Hank did because it really would not be fair to Hank to end up in a shelter for a long time," said Ryan. "And I don't even want to think about what would have happened if nobody wanted him after a while."

Ryan grew pensive, quietly licking his cone while they walked. But after a while, he continued. "Anyway, my Dad was good to his word. Turns out there was a kid about my age over on the other side of the state whose GenDog was hit by a car. So, Hank was a good age match, and my Dad gave them a good deal on buying Hank."

"Oh, that's good. I bet he misses you though. I know you miss him."

"Well, that's the odd part. I do miss Hank and especially did right after he left. But Hank seems to be doing just fine without me. I was able to do a FaceTime with the new family that has Hank. And Hank was cuddled up to the new kid like I never even existed. I think my Dad thought it would do me good to see Hank was OK, but it really kind of sucked to see how quick he moved on."

"Oh wow, that must have been hard. I am sorry Ryan."
Will was amazed though. He could not imagine Hunter
getting over him that easy. The year prior, when he left
town for a few days for a school trip, his Mom told him
Hunter just moped around and would not even eat.

Will realized that the relatively short life of a natural dog
might cut both ways. Will counted every year with Hunter
as special. But somehow perhaps Hunter also sensed that
his life was measured, that he was vulnerable to disease
and the lessening of aging. This vulnerability enhanced his
dependence on Will, but correspondingly also his unwav-
ering loyalty and devotion to his human. Both Will and
Hunter instinctively treasured their time together, a sense
that a GenDog might not have.

Both boys were quiet as they walked to the marina dock
and then checked out all of the boats. They could always
tell the local ones, modest aluminum skiffs but with good
reliable outboard motors that would guide the owners safely as they fished the Hood Canal and pulled and set crab
pots and shrimp pots. Nothing flashy, but they sure got the
job done. In contrast, the visiting boats were huge, hulk-
ing powerboats that sported all manner of downriggers
and electronic fish finders and cozy cabins, or sleek sailing
boats with gleaming teak trim that someone, likely, not
the owners, would have to spend copious hours keeping
varnished and shiny. The visitor boats all were prominently
labeled with names like "Emily Anne" or "Solace" or "My
Time", that either boasted of a woman in the owner's life

or sent some sort of message of how great the owner's life was, while the local boats were simply marked with state license numbers.

They continued to skip flat stones out into the bay, Hunter barking furiously and charging into the water to try to catch the ones that Will threw but usually only coming up with saltwater or eelgrass dripping from his snout. The boys' fun was interrupted by laughter from one of the moored powerboats, named the "Wave Catcher", and Will looked up to see a young teen girl with reddish-brown hair and green eyes that sparkled with humor standing on the bow. She wore petite white shorts and an oversized grey sweatshirt. Will was mesmerized – he could not remember ever seeing so cute of a girl. Come to think of it, he was not sure he had ever really seen a girl, at least not to be so aware that it was a girl and not just another kid.

"Your dog sure is trying hard!" shouted the girl. Will just stared back and dropped the rock that he was holding and ready to throw. Ryan looked at Will, immediately figured out what was going on, and answered back. "Yes, I guess my buddy is trying to turn his dog into a crab catcher! I am Ryan, and I don't remember seeing you around before."

"We just came for the weekend from up canal. So does your dog-training buddy have a name?"

Ryan nudged Will with an elbow to the side, which seemed to finally wake Will up.

"Hunter. No, I mean that is my dog. I'm Will. He's a really good hunter. I mean. On land he is. That's why I call him Hunter." Oh geez, thought Will, I am babbling.

"Hi Will, it looks like your dog is lots of fun. Well, see you around."

"We will?" asked Will.

"Sure, my Mom is working at the marina office now, so I suspect we'll be here most weekends until the weather gets too bad. Anyway, I have to go. But you might want to call your dog in, or get him a snorkel," said the girl as she pointed again to Hunter, still ducking his head under again and again trying to find just the right rock that Will threw.

"What's your name?" asked Will.

"Erin," answered the girl, with a wave as she ducked back into the cabin on her boat.

Will continued looking at the boat for a few moments longer, memorizing the site of Erin with her cute white shorts disappearing from view and figured he better try to get to know her better.

Chapter 25

Will and Erin climbed into his family's Kubota utility terrain vehicle. The two had been hanging out as often as possible on weekends when Erin traveled to town with her parents. Hunter moped about when Will went off with Erin, but today he was to keep them company. Will had promised to help his parents with the annual task of putting up firewood for the next winter. Every spring it took them a couple of months to cut and split enough wood to fill their shed so that it could finish seasoning and dry the rest of the spring, summer, and early fall. It was a necessary task, but one that Will thoroughly enjoyed. He did not want to shirk his responsibility in helping with this necessary effort, nor did he want to miss time with Erin.

"Just focus on the fallen fir tree up by the West property line, Will," said Dan. "It came down in that wind storm last spring, so it is pretty well seasoned. Your Mom and I bucked and cut it into fire log lengths yesterday. But we need you to haul all of it down here so we can split it up. Erin, thanks for helping, but you take care not to try to lift any pieces that are too large for you, OK?"

"Sure thing," said Erin. "I am just excited to see some more of the property. Will promised to show me some neat old-growth stumps today."

"Hunter, come!" said Will, as he pressed the fuel petal down on the UTV. It was a four-wheel-drive golf cart-like machine but with big knobby tires and a cargo bed on the back that could be raised to dump a load. It did not zip along quite as fast as a motorcycle, but Hunter loved to run with the Kubota almost as much as he loved to run with Will's motorcycle. Hunter surged on ahead but today Will was able to catch and keep up without maxing out the speed on the UTV.

"Hunter loves this, doesn't he?" said Erin. "He just hops and hops while he is running."

"He does. Don't you boy? Come on, let's go Hunter!" responded Will. "It's weird, usually I have trouble catching him on our 'Bota; it does not take off like my dirt bike. But today we are keeping right with him. I guess he is slowing down."

Will mused over this. He knew Hunter was not a puppy anymore. But he wasn't ready for Hunter to be approaching "middle-aged" and slowing down. He had way too many things he still wanted to do with his buddy.

"Hunter, this way!" Will called, steering his dog at each fork in the road. He brushed aside his worries. Will had today, with Hunter and Erin, and the sun was out. He could not help but be happy.

Soon they arrived at an area near the edge of the property with fairly mature trees. It had not been logged in 30 years or so, and the trees formed a dense forest canopy. Will stopped the Kubota and said "Come on Erin, you'll like this. It's one of my favorite places on our property." They stepped off of the road under the trees, treading on the soft ground made up of inches of spongy duff formed of fragrant needles and branches shed by the fir and hemlock trees overhead and bits of punky decayed wood, carpeted by layers of green moss through which primordial looking sword ferns sprouted here and there around the base of the trees. The area was crisscrossed by logs and branches from trees that had broken from the wind and were in various states of decay.

The moss carpet provided natural sound deadening as they walked among the trees and over downed trees, soft sun filtering down through the tree branches. Every so often a huge tree stump rose out of the duff, almost as tall as Will and Erin. These fir tree stumps were in an elegant state of decay, slabs of intact wood rising from or broken and spilling down from a punky decaying core, with mosses and huckleberry bushes growing from their sides, and sometimes a new, smaller fir tree having seeded on and growing right out of the original stump. As broken down as they were, you could see that each stump used to be a massive tree, over six feet across in diameter.

"Can you imagine what it would have looked like before they cut down the old-growth?" remarked Will. "I would love to have seen that. But wait until you see the cedars."

They continued down a rise to a low spot where rainwater and snowmelt gathered to form a shallow pond. It would be dry by summer but was currently filled a couple of feet deep with tobacco-colored water stained by red cedar fronds. A young bullfrog croaked a lonely refrain. The pond was surrounded by young cedar trees that were about two to three feet in diameter at their bases, enrobed in stringy brown bark and sporting sweeping green branches that dipped down low and then swooped back up in an arc.

"Wow, this is like Jurassic Park!" said Erin, awed by all of the mosses and ferns.

Reddish-orange cedar logs laid in the pond. The cedar wood was naturally preserved by chemicals that built up in cedar trees over time, giving it the characteristic red color and making it resistant to rot and insects. Also surrounding the ponds were majestic old-growth cedar stumps, six or even eight feet across. The bark had peeled off of these huge stumps many decades ago, but the wood remained pristine and looked as hard as it would have been when the trees were first cut for timber. The smooth wood was periodically grooved with vertical rivulets, giving the stumps a unique undulating look. And three or four feet up on each stump there were a series of horizontal notches.

"What are those holes on the stumps?" asked Erin, pointing to one of the notches? "They almost look like they were cut in by somebody."

"You're right, Erin," said Will. "Those are springboard notches. The loggers used to cut those into the base of a tree and then shove at the end of a board, which stuck out and made a shelf that the logger could perch on while he cut the tree. They cut trees with hand saws back then, and by getting a bit higher on the tree they did not have such a wide base to cut. Pretty cool that we can still see those, isn't it?"

"I would have loved to see those trees before they were cut." Erin could not help but think that as interesting as these old stumps were, they surely paled in comparison to what the old-growth must have been like. It's a shame that people had to destroy what they found, just because they could, she thought.

"Let's work our way back to the road," said Will. "We are close to that downed tree my parents cut up and need to get it loaded.

Will and Erin walked along contentedly, and Will was thrilled that Erin seemed to enjoy their time walking in the woods. He never could understand some of his friends that spent days like this inside playing video games. Will never minded the work of firewood cutting and collecting. As he neared the seasoned fir tree his parents had cut up, he smelled the sawdust, which instantly reminded him of a freshly cut two-by-four and an enjoyable deck construction project that he had helped his folks with. He loved everything about cutting firewood. Especially when they came across downed cedar logs, which when cut smelled like No. 2 pencils being sharpened. And if they were cutting fresh fir or hemlock, the air was redolent with an evergreen Christmas odor.

Erin helped Will pick up and move the firewood rounds, each about 18 inches long, to the cargo bed of the Kubota. Even though it was a cool day, they were both sweating and feeling loose from working their muscles. While they worked, Hunter dug about a series of holes in the duff, trying to scare out whatever he smelled that lived between the roots under tree stumps and in amongst the downed trees.

Will broke out a couple of pops and a bag of pretzels, shared by all, and it was time to take their load back to the cabin.

Chapter 26

As Will and Erin sat outside in the sun eating cones in front of the ice cream shop on a fine spring day, Hunter lay sprawled in the sun. While still in his prime, when the sun hit him just right like now, Will could see a few grey hairs creeping up his muzzle. As much as he enjoyed hanging out with Erin, Will had vowed to spend every minute he could with Hunter, and luckily Erin did not mind that the big dog tagged along everywhere they went.

Erin was just holding out the last of her vanilla cone to Hunter, who was slowly licking every sweet creamy drop from her hand when Karen McProbis came out of the store behind them.

"Hello Will, who is your friend?" asked the nosy woman.

"Oh, hi Mrs. McProbis. This is Erin."

"Are you new in town Erin?" asked Mrs. McProbis.

"Just visiting a lot. My mom works at the marina on the weekends," said Erin.

"Well, I see you are enjoying our little town. Just be careful who you hang out with, young lady," said Mrs. McProbis, with a tip of her head in Will's direction.

Erin picked up on the subtle slight. "Oh, I will, Mrs. McProbis. I will be sure to ask Will here which neighbors like to gossip and should be avoided."

Will snorted so hard he blew a bit of ice cream onto the sidewalk. Mrs. McProbis turned beet red and was trying to come up with a retort when her eye went to Hunter, busily licking up the ice cream splatter. Then she stared even harder and gave a triumphant grin. "Why Will, there sure looks to be grey on your mutt's muzzle. He's not a GenDog, is he? I knew there was something fishy about you and your dog."

Will grabbed Hunter's collar and pulled him close. "My Dad told you, he is a clone of my grandparent's dog."

"I remember him saying that. But funny thing is, I looked up the regulations, and the clone exception only applied to purebred dogs. Your dog is a mongrel, so that is not going to fly."

"What? You must be wrong Mrs. McProbis. I never heard that requirement. Now if you will excuse us, we will be on our way," said Will as he started to get up and urge Hunter and Erin along.

"Check it out online. Not even all the local CERT agents know the details since clones are so rare. But I am sure that the regional CERT Commander will be only too happy to inform the local agents once I let them know what is going on right under their noses."

"Mrs. McProbis, would you just leave us alone please?" asked Will, tugging on Hunter's collar. Hunter did not know what was going on, but he sensed his boy's stress, and let out a low growl.

"That's right boy, why don't you move along with that vicious mutt of yours. We will let the authorities sort this out." At this, Mrs. McProbis turned on her heel and stalked away purposefully.

Chapter 27

Will saw Erin home to her family's boat at the marina, then hustled out of town to where he had stashed his bicycle at the bottom of the road leading to their cabin. He started pedaling hard, wanting to go tell his parents what had just happened. Halfway home, at a point not really near anyone's house, he heard some barking off in the woods. Hunter heard it too, and his ears perked up. He turned to Will and let out a whine like he typically did when he wanted to go chase a deer or something.

"Not now Hunter, come on, we need to get right home." Will started back up on his bicycle and, for a while, Hunter kept up. But then that barking sound started again, and Hunter, with an apologetic look over his shoulder at Will, took off.

"Hunter! No! Come! We don't have time for this!" yelled Will. With a mix of both fear and anger, Will hopped off of his bike and took off into the woods after Hunter. But after fifteen minutes of futile trekking and calling, Will had to admit defeat and returned to his bike. He took some comfort in the fact that Hunter knew well the lay of the land. But he was concerned that Mrs. McProbis would send a CERT agent to nab Hunter.

Looking back over his shoulder and calling once in a while, Will continued on home.

But when he arrived, he saw that he was too late. A CERT truck sat in the driveway to their cabin. He saw Officer Rudey speaking with his father and walked over towards them. Dan spied Will and looked around and behind him with alarm. But he did not spot Hunter.

"Are you sure you do not have a natural dog here?" asked the CERT agent of Dan. "We received a very credible report that you were harboring a non-GenDog, non-clone, mongrel natural dog."

"As I told you, sir, there are no natural dogs here," answered Dan. "Whoever told you that had some bad information."

Officer Rudey looked dubiously at Dan and then around the property. Spying Will, he asked "What about you, Son? Have you seen a natural dog around?"

"No Sir," answered Will.

"You know that is a felony to knowingly harbor a prohibited natural dog?" asked the agent. "Why don't you tell me what's going on and I can make it go easier. For instance, if you did not know that a dog was a natural dog, we could get the charge reduced to a misdemeanor."

Officer Rudey waited while giving a stern eye to Will, but Will just shook his head again.

"Well, I will leave you for now," said the agent. "But I will be keeping an eye on you all." Officer Rudey stalked off, but then spied a bowl of dog kibble on the porch of the cabin.

Wheeling around, he pointed at the bowl. "What is that? I suppose that is dog food for your chickens? Come on, fess up!" shouted the agent at Dan.

"Congratulations. You found a bowl of cat food," replied Dan. "Now please leave our property unless you have a warrant."

The agent glared at Dan, kicked the bowl of dog kibble, spilling brown bits all over the porch, and stormed off. "I'll be back!" announced Officer Rudey, and roared off in his truck.

Will ran to Dan and hugged him. "Oh Dad, I saw Mrs. McProbis downtown and she said she was going to report Hunter. She must have done that. How are we going to keep Hunter safe?"

"We'll figure it out, Will. But where is Hunter? Did you hide him? I sure am glad he was not here."

"I don't know Dad. He heard some barking off in the woods and took off after it halfway up the hill. I am a little worried it might have been a coyote trying to lure him out."

"Well, he knows his way home, and how to handle the coyotes. Come on, let's go get some dinner."

Will and Dan filled Emma in on the day's events over dinner. Hunter had still not shown back home, but Will had refilled Hunter's bowl with fresh dog kibble and hoped he would show up before dark.

"Here is an idea," said Emma. "We have that wrought iron dinner bell on the front porch that we never use. Why don't we train Hunter to hide whenever we ring that? Then whenever one of us sees a CERT agent coming, we can ring the bell, and Hunter can go hide and be safe."

"Not a bad idea," answered Dan. "Will, why don't you take that on starting tomorrow? Assuming Hunter comes home by then."

Just as if he had been summoned by that statement, they heard Hunter's claws on the porch and a scratch on the front door.

"Hunter! I knew you would come back!" exclaimed Will as he flung open the door. Hunter stood there thumping his tail and licked Will's face excitedly. But when Will called him in, instead of coming in immediately, Hunter looked over his shoulder towards the edge of the woods. Will spied a thin medium-sized reddish dog with a white blaze on its head peeking out from the woods, which gave a yip in Hunter's direction. Hunter woofed in return and then looked expectantly as if he was waiting for the dog to join him. But the other dog just stared, then turned and disappeared back into the woods.

Hunter started after the other dog until Will called "Come on Hunter, not again." Will shook the dog food bowl. "Come inside for dinner, boy." Hunter paused, clearly torn, but aided by the proximity of his boy and the tantalizing smell of roasted chicken wafting from the cabin ultimately turned and followed Will inside.

Hunter was ravenous and emptied his food bowl twice, as well as eating all the scraps he could mooch from the family.

"Where have you been old boy?" asked Emma as she scratched Hunter under the chin and stared into his deep brown eyes. "Did you make a new friend? I bet she is something special."

"She?" asked Will. "Why do you say 'she'. Do you think that red dog was a girl dog?"

"Will, how do you feel when you see Erin?"

Will did not answer, but made a choking sound and blushed deeply, staring down into his lap.

"I thought so," said Emma. "Do you like her enough to want to follow her if you see her around town? I am guessing that is how Hunter feels about that other dog and why he was gone all day."

Dan laughed and reached over to pet Hunter. "So, we have a couple of Romeos, do we? Well, you boys have work to do tomorrow, learning how to respond to that dinner bell. Best you get off to sleep."

Chapter 28

It did not take long for Hunter to learn what Will wanted. Will would ring the dinner bell, and Hunter would run to the barn and hide behind a pile of hay bales. Will would leave a piece of cheese behind the hay bales as a reward. It took a few more days for Hunter to understand that the same response was called for when Dan or Emma rang the bell, but soon they were practicing daily and Hunter would reliably go hide every time.

The whole family felt satisfied with the arrangement and soon everything went back to normal. Well, almost normal. Hunter no longer made trips into town with any of them. And they practiced weekly "hide Hunter" drills using the dinner bell.

Will and Hunter continued roaming the hillside above the family's cabin, on foot, bicycle and motorcycle. It seemed the duo never ran short of places to explore, and Erin sometimes kept them company. They never saw other dogs but knew that Hunter had at least one friend somewhere out there.

One June evening, Will and Hunter were making their way home for a late barbecue dinner. That time of year it could stay light until ten o'clock in the evening and it was easy to lose track of time. As they came closer the smell of grilling meat wafted in the air, and Hunter surged ahead to the house. With a stroke of unfortunate timing, a CERT truck pulled up in front of the house just as Hunter burst out from the woods. Emma was flipping chicken breasts on the grill but saw the truck and turned, ran up the porch, and rang the dinner bell long and loud. Hunter skidded in his tracks and turned toward the barn, pivoting on his back paws while continuing forward into the barn. He was so fast! But not fast enough.

The CERT agent, Officer Rudey, spied Hunter as the dog ducked into the barn, and yelled "Halt! Stop you dog!"

Everything happened so fast. The agent started running towards the barn. Dan had heard the commotion and came around from the side of the cabin and also ran for the barn. Will heard the dinner bell just as he was about to break out of the woods behind Hunter, and stopped in the shadows to see what was going on.

"What are you doing on our property?" demanded Dan of the agent, standing in front of the barn door which he luckily had reached a few steps ahead of the officer. Will's father stood statue-like, his arms folded resolutely over his chest. Will observed all of this and, still staying in the cover of the trees, crept around behind the barn. He found a loose siding board and lifted it, calling softly for Hunter. "Hunter, come," he whispered. He was gratified with an immediate response, Hunter poking his head out and licking Will's face. "Come on boy, let's go." Hunter came out the rest of the way and, after Will replaced the loose board, the pair melted back into the woods.

Officer Rudey and Dan could not see Will and Hunter but Emma, from her vantage point on the porch, saw them slinking off. She breathed a sigh of relief and headed for the barn.

"Move aside," said the CERT agent to Dan. "I saw a mutt run into your barn. We told you we would be keeping an eye on you all. Now I want to see inside your barn."

"Not without a warrant," answered Dan firmly.

"You mean like this one?" sneered Officer Rudey, holding up an official-looking document for Dan to inspect.

Dan started reading the warrant when Emma reached the pair. She rested a hand on Dan's shoulder. "It's OK Dan, let the man in. We have nothing to hide."

Dan turned to Emma with a surprised look on his face. She gave him a subtle nod, letting him know it was OK. "I don't know why you keep harassing us. But if seeing inside the barn will help convince you that there is no natural dog here, go for it."

"I know what I saw," said the agent. "And it sure looked like a dog running into your barn. Time to put a stop to this foolishness."

"You must have seen one of the chickens," said Emma. "But have a look around."

Officer Rudey brushed past Dan and burst into the barn. He could see fairly well with the filtered sun shining in from a dusty window and light streaming in through the open door, with dust motes swirling in the sun's rays. And he saw no dog anywhere, and nothing that looked like a dog. But he knew he had seen one run in, so soon he was holding up his tactical flashlight and shining it into every nook and cranny of the barn, including behind the stack of hay bales. He found lots of dusty equipment, sacks of feed, and a random couple of hens making nests in loose straw, but no dog.

Admitting defeat, a frustrated agent left the barn and. While not quite apologizing, thanked Dan and Emma gruffly for their cooperation.

He climbed back into his truck, sat looking long and hard at the barn and Will's parents, and then called someone on his radio. With that, he gave a satisfied nod of his head and went on his way.

Chapter 29

Will decided it was best if he stayed away from the cabin for a while, and went walking in the opposite direction with Hunter. He was worried but knew that it was not safe to go home. Hunter could sense his tension, and kept looking to Will for reassurance and a pat.

After thirty minutes or so, Will stopped and called Erin on his cell phone. "Hey Erin, I won't be able to hang out tonight. Something has come up."

"That's OK," answered Erin. "Is everything alright?"

"I hope so," answered Will, not ready to explain all that was troubling him, at least not over the phone. "I just need to make sure Hunter is OK."

"That reminds me," said Erin. "I just saw a CERT helicopter passing overhead, and it was heading in the direction of town."

"A helicopter?" asked Will. "At this time of night? That's odd." Just then Will began to hear the distant thrumming of a chopper, and it was growing louder. "Hey, thanks for the heads up. I have to go," said Will as he abruptly hung up and pocketed his phone.

"Come on Hunter, we need to go deeper into the woods." The two started again when Will's phone vibrated in his pocket. He looked at it and rapidly answered, "Mom? Do we still have to hide Hunter?"

"Yes, Will. You did a great job in getting Hunter out of the barn, and we chased that agent off," answered Emma. "But he just came back with Officer Devus. And this time they have a tracker with them. They are over behind the barn looking at the dirt."

"Did you see a helicopter go overhead?"

"I heard one, yes."

"Erin said she saw a CERT logo on it."

"Go, hide. Put your phone on silent. But call me if you need anything."

"Thanks, Mom. I love you."

"I love you too," said Emma, her voice breaking. "Take care of Hunter, but stay safe, OK? Your Dad and I will come to find you later."

With that Will and Hunter started running. They knew they needed to get under the cover of big trees so that the helicopter would not see them. And to elude the tracker, they needed water. All of this screamed to Will: head to the cedar pond!

Will and Hunter went surging forward, zig-zagging between trees and jumping downed logs. As they went deeper into the woods and slightly downhill towards the pond, they heard the helicopter drawing closer. The boy and dog made it under the thick canopy provided by the cedar boughs just in time, disappearing into a sea of green when viewed from overhead.

As soon as the chopper passed over, Will and Hunter sprang back into action and started wading into the pond. They worked their way through the coppery tannic acid-shaded water and across to the other side. They then worked their way down a stream that flowed down a ravine from the pond, hoping all of the water would be enough to drown out their scents.

Will and Hunter then jumped on a fallen hemlock log that crossed the stream and followed it across the bottom of the ravine to the distant hillside. Scrambling as fast as they could up the slope, the pair then darted into a loamy hollow under a gnarled old fir log. They hunkered low under the overhanging grey-green moss as Will tried not to think about how many beetles might be crawling around in the rubble of the damp punk wood that lined the hole in which they sheltered. "Shhh, Hunter," whispered Will, drawing his dog in close. Hunter reacted to the stress emanating from Will, understanding on an instinctive level that there was some threat approaching. The dog nuzzled his soft nose and velvety whiskers into the crook of Will's neck, and Will stroked his damp, mottled brown fur. Each calmed the other as their breathing slowed and, finally, Will thought they were safe.

But then the still air was disturbed by the crack of a branch breaking just a short distance away, across the stream on the opposite hillside. Will and Hunter pressed down still further into the damp earth, trying not to make a sound. The boy thought feverishly of how he could defend Hunter if they were found. The rustle of leaves and crackling of fallen branches from across the ravine told him a CERT tracker was drawing close.

Peering out, Will spied the tracker approach the cedar pond. The uniformed man started working his way in a circle around the pond. Every once in a while, he held up a little device from which a tube projected that seemed to sniff the air, tapped a button on the device, and frowned at a display on it. Completing his circle, the man stood at a muddy spot where he started and keyed a mic clipped to a strap on his shoulder. Will could not make out what the man said, but saw him shaking his head and frowning as he spoke into the mic. The tracker then took a last look around, scanning the hillside in both directions, causing Will to press down further than he thought possible under the log, with one arm firmly on Hunter's back and the other holding Hunter's muzzle.

Will could make out the sounds of the man moving across the forest floor again, but things echoed around so much he could not be certain of the direction in which he was moving. Feeling along the ground, Will's hand seized upon a fist-sized rock that he grasped in his hand on the other side of Hunter. He did not want to use it but would do what he could to defend his beloved companion.

Time crept by, and Will kept waiting for someone to peer at him under the log. After what seemed like an hour, during which Will and Hunter stayed frozen, the boy's legs started cramping up. He cautiously peeked his head out and was relieved to see nobody. Relaxing somewhat, Will remained in his hidey-hole and slowly stroked Hunter's coat to keep him calm.

Chapter 30

Dan and Emma waited anxiously throughout the evening, hoping that Will and Hunter would be safe. The hillside behind their cabin was alive with several aluminum-colored helicopters flying in a grid-like pattern while shining large spotlights on the ground. The air was rent with the sound of four-wheelers peeling through the hills, radio static, and the occasional gunshot.

As the twilight grew, a line of vehicles, headlights blazing, could be seen snaking down the hill on a forest service road and the helicopters finally bore off towards town. When the trucks passed the cabin, one peeled off and pulled into Dan and Emma's driveway. Officer Rudey exited the passenger seat of the cab and waved Dan and Emma over.

"I want to show you folks something," said Officer Devus as he opened the back of the truck. Inside were four cages, three of which were occupied by dogs. Upon seeing the agent, each of the dogs pressed timidly into the backs of their cages. Noting their matted fur, stinking of urine and fear, Emma thought that she had never seen such desolate creatures. The agent shined his light on the furthest cage, illuminating a dog that had dirty brown fur, a mud-stained tawny mask, and white tips on its paws. Emma gasped audibly and sagged into Dan.

"I thought so!" said Officer Rudey. "She's your dog, isn't she?"

Puzzled, Emma thought a moment, peering carefully at the dog before responding. "Wait, you found this girl dog up there?" gesturing towards the hillside.

"We sure did," said the agent, as he poked the dog in the cage and was rewarded by a snarl and low growl. "She put up quite a fight! So, she's your mutt, isn't she?"

"Nope, we have never seen her before," said Emma.

"I told you before, mister, we don't have a wild dog," said Dan.

"Even with the evidence staring you here in the face, you can't do the right thing and admit this is your dog?" said the agent. "Boy. Some people will do anything to avoid a fine. But it doesn't matter to me, even if we can't prove she is yours, we have the cur either way. And believe me, she won't be causing any more problems where she is going."

With that, Officer Rudey gave Dan a last glare, slammed the back of the truck closed, and sped off.

The night air grew cool and Will could no longer hear any helicopters hovering. Still, he remained hidden. They were both cold and hungry, but the boy was paralyzed with fear that he would show himself too early and endanger Hunter.

As the evening gloom darkened, Will spied a pair of lights traveling down the opposite hillside towards the pond. Will tensed up, convinced he had been right to stay hidden, and tried again to find the rock he had somehow dropped while weighing whether he should make a break for it. But then he heard his name carried on the wind. It was his parents, calling him over and over. "Will! It's OK, you can come out now!"

Relieved beyond measure, Will stood and stretched his aching limbs, as Hunter did the same, followed by a shake of his coat to remove bits of dirt and fir needles. "Mom! Dad! We're over here!"

Will powered up his phone and turned on the flashlight app, and started making his way down to the pond to meet his parents. "You found us! Are you sure it is OK for Hunter to come out now?" asked Will.

Emma hugged Will close while Dan rubbed both sides of Hunter's head and told him what a good boy he was. "We had a feeling you would head to the pond; it seems like it has been a favorite spot of yours for as long as we can remember," answered Emma. "And yes, it is safe, the CERT agents are gone, as are the helicopters."

"I am surprised they gave up. Do you think they will come back?" asked Will.

"I don't think they will be back, Will," answered Dan, giving his son a long hug.

Will noticed that Dan did not look happy though. "How can you be sure?"

"Well, they captured three wild dogs. They brought them by our cabin in cages in the back of a truck. And one of them looked a lot like Hunter, but it was a girl dog. Maybe one of his littermates."

"What will happen to those wild dogs?" asked Will.

Emma gave Dan a sad look. She hated that her son had to learn such things about the world, but felt he was old enough to know the truth. "The dogs I saw were terrified and pressed hard against the insides of their cages. It's not the way any living creature should be treated. I do not know for certain, but I think that CERT will put those dogs down. Which is a real shame. They have done nothing wrong and just want a chance to live their lives. I am so sorry, Will."

Will looked at his parents with tears in his eyes. He wasn't surprised by his Mom's answer; he had suspected it to be the case. "I can't help but think that what is happening to those dogs could be happening to Hunter. I am relieved that it is not. But that's not fair, is it? Those dogs are just as full of life as Hunter. How can they just put them down? Can we do anything to help them? There must be something we can do."

"I wish there was, Will. And we can try. We can call our legislators and demand that this kind of thing stops. There are enough like-minded people that maybe we can get this craziness turned around."

"But that will take time. What about the dogs that were captured today? What about Hunter's sister?"

Dan broke in. "Let's give it some thought Will. But right now, why don't we get home and give you and Hunter some dinner. Hunter should be safe for now because CERT thinks they already caught him."

Chapter 31

Nobody slept well that night. It was true, Hunter was safe. And if they could keep him out of town, he should stay that way, as CERT believed he had already been caught. But Will and his parents all spent a sleepless night thinking about the poor creatures cowering in the CERT cages.   how much life and potential each of those wild dogs held because Hunter had been one. It was just so unfair that the other dogs would not have the same chance at life as Hunter.

Emma was the first to get up and went down to the kitchen to make a cup of tea. As she sat sipping her chamomile, she heard a step on the stairs, and then Dan appeared. "You couldn't sleep either, eh?" said Emma as Dan came up behind her and rubbed her shoulders.

"There has to be a better way," said Dan. "Who are we, the human race, to say which animals deserve to live and which should die? I know the CERT act was well-intended but could the animal lovers that passed it comprehend what CERT agents would be doing today? They would not be sleeping either if they did."

"I would like to put those agents in cages," said Will from the stairwell.

"Come on in Will, how about I make some hot chocolate?" said Emma, to which both Dan and Will nodded in agreement.

The family sat sipping hot chocolate. "Sometimes when a thing feels wrong, it is," said Dan resolutely. "And sometimes when something that is supposed to be wrong feels right, it is."

"What do you mean, Dad?" asked Will.

"Why don't we go for a drive and check out the CERT facility. It should be pretty quiet this time of night," said Dan. "It might be best if you kept Hunter here, Emma." Will could not believe what he thought his father had in mind and decided not to ask too many more questions.

Emma looked at Dan with a proud smile, nodded, and said "Come on boy, you had enough excitement for the night." She led Hunter into the living room and sat down on the couch. Hunter joined her, curled up in a ball, and pressed in tight.

On their way out to the truck, Dan detoured to the barn and came out with a crowbar. The two climbed into the truck and drove away.

Dan stopped the truck a block away from but in sight of the back of the CERT building and retrieved a flashlight out of the glove box. "I want you to stay here, Will," he said as he set his cell phone to "vibrate" and picked up the crowbar from under the seat. "Send me a text if you see anyone or notice any lights come on in that building."

"Dad, I want to come. Those dogs need our help."

"I know, son. And that's what we are going to do. But I don't want you getting into trouble that will cause you problems later in life. I have this. Now stay here and keep a close eye out."

Will watched his father walk to the CERT building. The lower floor of the building was sturdily built of solid concrete. A set of metal double doors inset in the concrete opened onto a loading dock stripped with yellow paint lines. The doors were closed, and all was quiet and dark. There was enough moonlight to see his father test the doors, which did not budge. Will watched Dan look around furtively, then drive the end of his crowbar into the door jamb next to the lock. It took a few tries, but he soon managed to pry it open, with one of the doors swinging out and hitting the concrete with a loud "bang" that made Will cringe. His father then disappeared inside the building.

Will held his breath but did not see any immediate re-action. He could occasionally see glimpses of his father's flashlight bobbing around inside through the open door.

Suddenly, a light came on upstairs on the second floor of the building. Will hurriedly texted his father "Get out! Someone heard you!" But he could not make out any reaction from his father. He texted again "Get out now!"

There was still no reaction, and Will reasoned that the concrete might be blocking his father's phone signal. He noticed more lights coming on upstairs. Making a fast decision, Will opened the truck door and ran for the building.

Will poked his head in through the door. All was dark, but he heard some whimpering coming from the other end of a long, gloomy hallway. He crept down the hall, using the flashlight app on his phone to light the way.

At the end of the hall, Will spied his Dad's flashlight shining from an open door. Ducking in, he saw a wall lined with stainless steel cages stacked like cordwood. His Dad was staring at a stainless surgical table in the center of the room that had several open Velcro straps hanging from it. Shelves below the table housed stacks of plastic-sealed syringes and vials of drugs. A large black plastic tote on wheels stood next to the table.

"Dad! We've been found out! There are people upstairs, we have to go!" said Will in an urgent whisper.

Dan turned his flashlight beam from the table to the cages, and Will could see that a half dozen of those each held a dog. The dogs were crouched down, pressed low and staring back at Dan and Will in fear.

"Will, you should have stayed in the truck," responded Dan. "But since you are here, help me get these cages open. I could never live with myself if we left these pitiful creatures to their fate."

"Yes, let's hurry!" answered Will. With that, Will and Dan each moved to the first cage and figured out how to open the latch. A mangy German Shepherd-looking dog stared back at them from the back of the cage, growling in fear. The air was redolent of urine produced by the terrified animals. "Come on boy, you are free!" said Will, as he flung the cage door open, but the untrusting dog did not move.

The pair then moved on to the next cage. As soon as they moved, the first dog realized its way was not blocked and jumped down, letting out a loud bark.

"We better hurry now!" exclaimed Dan. The two moved from cage to cage, opening them to a growing crescendo of excited barking as the dogs realized what was happening. Will noticed one of the cages held a dog that looked a lot like Hunter but was smaller, and another held a red-colored dog with a white blaze on its head that looked like Hunter's girlfriend.

Soon Will, Dan, and a pack of dogs were all running for the door, as they heard loud pounding coming from a nearby stairwell. "Stop! Stop! What are you doing?" they heard just as they burst out of the building. They recognized the voice of Officer Devus behind them but ignored him completely.

The father and son did not stop, racing for the truck as the dogs all disappeared into the night. They leaped into the truck and Dan gunned the engine as they sped away with their headlights off. Lights were coming on in the parking lot and street, but the truck made it out before it could be well lit up.

"I can't believe it! We did it!" shouted Will gleefully.

"Yes, we did!" said Dan, high-fiving his son. "Now please don't take this as permission to always break the rules. But some rules have to be broken to do what is right, and this was one. Let's keep this to the family though, OK? Not even Ryan or Erin should hear about this, right?"

"You bet Dad. Thanks for helping out those dogs. What a night!"

Back home, a sleeping Hunter perked up and stared at the door. He jumped down from the couch, went and stood nose to the door, whined, and looked at Emma.

"Time to go out boy?" said Emma as she stood up to let Hunter out. When she opened the door, she heard the baying of multiple dogs running up the hillside, and Hunter took off after them.

"Hunter, wait!" shouted Emma, as she watched Hunter disappear with several other dogs passing by through the edge of the woods. Sighing and smiling, Emma shook her head. "Well, I might as well make some grilled cheese. I bet I am going to have some hungry, trouble-making boys here soon."

Chapter 32

THREE YEARS LATER

The faded red pickup bumped along as Will worked the gears to climb up to the cabin, with Erin snuggled on the front seat alongside him. Once they crested the last hill and the cabin came into view, Hunter jumped down from the cabin porch and trotted over to meet the truck.

"Is Hunter limping?" asked Erin, as the big dog shoved his head into her hand for a pet.

"Yeah, he has been doing that for a while now. It doesn't seem to slow him down though. He still heads out to run the woods and play with his dog friends."

Erin finished climbing down from the truck cab, but before she could close the door Hunter jumped up on the seat next to Will.

"So, you want to go, do you?" laughed Will. "I sure miss taking you with me, boy." Will had not been able to take Hunter into town the past three years, ever since that big dog round-up when Hunter was almost caught.

"Do you mind if we take Hunter for a hike before we start practicing for tomorrow's history exam?" asked Will.

"Of course not!" answered Erin. "You know I never miss out on a chance to hang with my favorite boys."

"Let's go, Hunter!" said Will. The dog thumped his tail and jumped out of the truck, but let out a yelp when he landed on both forepaws and collapsed to the ground. Hunter immediately scrambled to his feet, yet held his left front leg up gingerly.

"Hey boy, what's going on?" asked Will softly, as he felt Hunter's leg. It seemed to move just fine, but he noted that the knee joint was swollen and warm. "Come on, let's see what my Mom thinks." The three went up to the cabin, Hunter limping but still wagging his tail, happy to be with the people he loved.

Once inside, Emma examined Hunter's leg. "This is worrisome, Will. If it had just started, I would think he sprained his knee and we should just let Hunter rest. But he's been limping for a while now, hasn't he?" asked Emma.

"Yes, about a month. But never this bad," answered Will. "Jumping out of the truck just now seems to have aggravated things."

"We should probably get him checked out by a vet," said Emma.

"But I thought it was not safe to take Hunter anywhere that he might be seen," worried Will. "We have done a really good job of keeping him away from town."

"I think we can trust Dr. McKay," answered Emma. "You remember her, right? The one that stitched up Hunter after that cougar attack? Why don't I give her a call and see if we can take him in?"

Emma left for the kitchen and dialed up the vet's office. Will heard his Mom leave a cryptic message asking for Dr. McKay to call back about a sick dog, without leaving any details. Then she put together an ice pack and went back to the living room to sit with Hunter, Will, and Erin. They iced Hunter's sore leg and waited for Dr. McKay to call them back.

Will and his parents drove to the back of the veterinary clinic that night. It was after hours, but Dr. McKay came to the door to meet them when they pulled up. "Come on in, quickly now," said Dr. McKay as she herded the group into the back of the clinic's kennel area. Once they were inside, she turned on the lights.

"Hey boy, it's good to see you!" said Dr. McKay as she knelt to pet Hunter. "I thought Hunter was caught a few years ago. I sure was surprised to receive your call today, Emma."

"Thanks for seeing us Dr. McKay," said Emma. 'We've had to keep Hunter out of sight. I am sure you understand why."

"I do indeed," said the vet. "The local CERT field agents kind of went a little crazy after all the dogs they caught that one night somehow escaped. They combed the town and foothills for days trying to find them all. I know they did find some. But not your big guy, I take it. Good!"

Dr. McKay squatted down to pet Hunter. "So, what's going on big guy?" she asked, as Hunter beat a rhythm on the floor with his tail while licking the vet's chin. Dr. McKay felt along the length of each of the dog's legs, pausing when she felt a warm swelling on his left front. She flexed Hunter's leg at each of the joints, noting the way they moved. The dog whimpered a bit as she flexed his knee. "Let's get you an X-ray and see if what can find out what is going on in there, OK?"

The vet walked Hunter back into the surgery and asked the family to wait. It was not long before she walked the dog back, who was overjoyed to see Will, Dan, and Emma. They each looked expectantly at Dr. McKay, who had a somber demeanor. "I am afraid I have some bad news," said the vet. She clipped an x-ray film plate onto the front of a viewer on the wall.

At first blush, the leg x-ray looked normal to the family. "It doesn't look like anything is broken, does it?" asked Will, staring at the images.

"No, nothing is broken. But do you see this white area on the distal end of his femur?" Dr. McKay pointed to the lower end of Hunter's long thigh bone. "And you see how the bone flares out extra-wide there, compared to the proximal end of the lower leg bones that meet it to form the stifle joint?"

"You mean his knee?" asked Will.

"Yes, that's right. The stifle joint is his knee. And the lower end of his big bone here is swollen, which makes his knee hurt when he moves it." Will looked closer at the image and noted that the swollen area of the bone had little irregular roundish shapes in it, which looked different from the uniform appearance of the other bones.

"How do we fix that swelling?" asked Dan. "Do we need to give him anti-inflammatories, like aspirin, and rest?"

"I wish it were that simple" answered Dr. McKay. "Do you see those irregular shapes in the swollen bone end? Those are clumps of tumor cells. I am afraid your dog has osteosarcoma or bone cancer."

"Cancer?" asked Emma. "But he has always been so healthy. Why he was running without any problems just last week." She unconsciously leaned up against and held Hunter close as she talked.

"I have not seen bone cancer in dogs for a few years now. It used to be pretty common in some large breeds, like boxers, golden retrievers, German shepherds, and Rottweilers," explained Dr. McKay. "But they engineered out the genes that cause cancers from GenDogs, so we don't see it anymore."

"How do we treat it?" asked Dan. "I have friends that had a dog with cancer years ago, and they did surgery and then chemotherapy. Could we do that? I know it would be expensive, but maybe we could have a payment plan?"

"I wish it were only a matter of money," answered the vet. "They don't make dog chemotherapeutics anymore, due to lack of demand. And even if they did, we would have to first do surgery to remove the tumor. Which in this case would be removing Hunter's sick leg."

"An amputation?" asked Emma. "Oh wow, that would be hard on Hunter, wouldn't it?"

"Three-legged dogs can do just fine if they are small," responded Dr. McKay. "But Hunter is a pretty good-sized dog. It would be a lot of suffering to put him through, and he would at best limp around afterward. Without chemotherapy, there is a good chance that cancer would come roaring back in a few months."

"So that's it? We are just going to give up on Hunter?" said an anguished Will, angry and struggling with tears at the same time. "We don't need to sit here then, come on boy!" Will huffed out with Hunter in tow.

Dan and Emma apologized to Dr. McKay and thanked her again for her discretion in seeing Hunter at night. "I get it," said Dr. McKay. "The boy's upset; I would be too if it were my dog."

"How long do we have?" asked Dan.

"Maybe a month," answered the vet. "Watch him for pain. I will send him home with something for that, and you can get refills from me when needed. Eventually, it won't work. You'll know when the time comes, and I will also provide a packet of meds for that time."

Chapter 33

Will and his family enjoyed Hunter's companionship even more, if that was possible, over the next two months. Hunter and Will went up into the hills each morning, sometimes accompanied by Erin, though their wanderings became shorter and shorter every day. And the old boy still took off in the evenings sometimes, to visit with his canine companions, after which he would come back limping but with his tongue happily lolling.

Eventually, Hunter was content to lay on the front porch and watch his family go to and from, though you could tell it stressed him not to be able to follow them everywhere they went. Emma made sure Hunter had a pain pill three times a day, but by the end of summer had to increase the dosage to a point that Hunter slept a lot. With help from Will to lift him up, and later down, Hunter curled up with the young man in his bed every night. Will had come to accept the situation but dreaded that his time with his dear Hunter might soon come to an end. He could not imagine life without his best friend.

One grey fall morning, Will awoke to the sound of rain pelting the metal roof, and reached over to pet Hunter.

The dog was drawing ragged, shaky breaths, something Will had not noticed before. He tried to get Hunter up to go outside, but the dog could not raise himself off of the bed. Slipping out of bed, he went to find his Mom, who was making coffee in the kitchen. "Something is wrong with Hunter," said Will.

The two went to check out their beloved dog, who thumped his tail on the bed covers to see them but was clearly in distress. Emma looked hard into Hunter's watery eyes. "I think it's time, Will," said Emma. "He looks like he is suffering this morning." Will did not answer but continued to stroke his dog's head as tears streamed down his face.

"You understand what is happening, don't you Will?" asked Emma. Will nodded and swallowed. "I don't want him to suffer," he choked out. "I'll be back soon," said Emma.

Emma went to find Dan and filled him in on the situation. "I don't want to stress Hunter with another trip into town, and I also don't think we should wait until late at night to go to Dr. McKay's," said Emma.

"What choice do we have?" asked Dan. "I will do anything I can to help that dog out."

"Do you remember the packet that Dr. McKay gave us?" asked Emma. Dan nodded yes. "We could use that. I don't want to, but I will do that for him."

Emma found the packet from Dr. McKay, pulled out the meds, ground them up and mixed them with some leftover chicken and gravy from the refrigerator.

Dan helped Will lift and carry Hunter to lay in front of a crackling fire in their wood stove. The family gathered around their dear dog and took turns petting and holding him, and telling him through their tears what a good boy he was. Hunter looked at them all with love in his eyes, and then happily lapped up the meat and medication concoction. Emma felt an uncommon mixture of emotions, part love, part guilt, and sorrow, as she helped Hunter enjoy his last meal.

Hunter's ragged breathing grew smooth as his pain disappeared and, with the last lick of Will's hand and thump of his tail, he closed his eyes and drifted off.

Will and Erin stood with their arms around each other's waists, as did Emma and Dan, around the freshly mounded dirt on the hillside below a cedar tree behind the cabin. The sun had broken out and, from their vantage point, they could see the cabin and surrounding Christmas tree fields. "Hunter will be able to watch over us all from here," said Dan. "He sure was a good dog."

"That dog brought me so much joy for so many years," said Will. "But I didn't know how much it would hurt when we had to say goodbye."

"That's the thing about life, son," said Dan. "The highs and the lows go together. It's the people and things that we love the most that can also cause us the most pain. But what would life be without them?"

Chapter 34

The Halloween decorations that Emma put up on the porch railing were not successful in dispelling the pall that had persistently hung, like honey that had partially crystallized, around the cabin the last two months. Will, in particular, seemed to have lost his spark, and could not get thoughts of Hunter out of his head. He missed him when he woke up and found nobody to pet, when he finished his dinner and found himself saving the last bite until he remembered that there was nobody to give it to, and when he walked in the woods and heard a creature breaking branches and looked up expectantly before he recalled that his good boy would not be careening onto the path.

Dan had offered to buy Will a discounted GenDog, one of those that had been turned back into CERT when something unexpected happened to their matched owners. Even though Will knew that rescuing a returned GenDog might save it from an uncertain future if no new match could be found, it just wasn't the same. His relationship with Hunter was special and Will did not think he could ever love another dog like he had Hunter. And certainly not a GenDog, whose engineered perfection made it imperfect in Will's eyes.

And now there had been another wild dog round-up last night. The trucks and helicopters had been busy for hours, and it depressed Will, even more, to think of how many good dogs had been hunted down. Perhaps even Hunter's girlfriend had been caught. The whole situation was just so unfair.

Erin broke into Will's musings. "Come on, Will," she said. "Let's go out for a walk in the woods. Maybe go down to the cedar pond? It will do you some good."

"I suppose you are right," replied Will. "I have not been to the pond since we lost Hunter. He loved splashing about in that water so much. Too many memories for me."

"Well, Hunter would still want you to go enjoy it. He was all about grabbing the joy in every moment, without thinking about what had happened the day prior or what might happen tomorrow."

The two made their way down to the pond and sat under the cedar fronds watching a pair of ducks swimming and occasionally diving for small fish. Will had his arm around Erin, who laid back on his chest. "It's still pretty magical here, isn't it?" asked Erin.

"I suppose so," answered Will. "Hunter and I had some good times here. And we hid up on that hillside across the pond the night of that first round up."

"Do you think they caught more dogs last night?" asked Erin.

Will did not answer for some time. Then was about to say he hoped not when he stopped and listened hard. "Did you hear that?"

"I did," answered Erin. "It sounded like some whimpering coming from across the pond. I don't hear it now though. Maybe it was just two trees rubbing together in the wind."

The two sat and listened further and, all of a sudden, the wind shifted and they heard it again. "There is some animal over there that is lost or hurt – let's go check it out!" said Will.

The two raced around the pond to the other side and then stopped and listened until they heard the sound again. They did this periodically until they came to a hollow in an earthen bank that was overhung by a downed, moss-covered tree and sheltered by ferns and branches covering its opening. They could hear the whimpering now, which stopped whenever they made noise but then started again after a moment.

Will and Erin dropped to their knees and peered into the hollow. They could not quite make out what they were seeing, so Erin pulled out her cell phone and turned on its flashlight app.

"Oh wow, they are so small!" whispered Erin. Looking back at her were two puppies. One was brown and had one ear folded over and one ear stuck halfway up. The second puppy was reddish and had a white stripe on its head. "Hey. Do you think…?" asked Erin.

"Yup, they sure look like Hunter and his girlfriend," answered Will. "I guess the old boy wanted to make sure we were not lonely!"

The little red puppy crawled over to Erin, grabbed her pinky finger, and started to suck. "Looks like they are hungry!" laughed Erin.

"Maybe CERT caught their Mamma?" said Will. "Let's take them home and get them some food." With that, he reached in to grab the brown puppy, which let out a cute little growl and nipped his hand. "Wow, aren't you a brave one!" laughed Will, scooping the puppy up. Despite his bravado, the puppy found itself snuggling into Will's shirt.

"Mom, Dad, look what we found!" shouted Will excitedly as he and Erin burst into the cabin. He put the two pups into Hunter's old bed by the woodstove, which seemed huge for such small creatures. The pups wrestled each other a bit but then started making a mewling sound.

"What dears! And that one looks just like a miniature of Hunter. And he's even a boy!" exclaimed Emma. "But it sounds like they are hungry! Let me see if I can fix up some warm milk to feed them with an eyedropper."

"That other one, the little red female, looks a lot like one of the dogs we freed a few years ago, Will," said Dan.

"Yes, she looks like the girl dog I saw Hunter hanging out with," said Will. As they talked the little girl dog crawled its way over to Erin and again started to suck on her pinkie. Will picked up the boy dog, which this time recognized a friend and tried to suck on the drawstring of his sweatshirt.

"It sure appears that they like you two," said Dan.

"And I bet after you feed them, they will like you," said Emma, who came back in with the warm milk.

"Dad, Mom, can I keep this little guy?" asked Will, as he fed the male pup.

"And if it's OK with my folks, can I keep this little one?" asked Erin, holding the female pup close as it suckled on a dropper.

Emma looked at Dan and they both smiled. It was great to see Will so full of life again. "Of course, Will," answered Emma. "Erin, I know your folks are sympathetic to wild dogs. I expect they will be fine as well. But if they are not for any reason, she can stay here."

"But what should we do to find these pups' mamma?" asked Will. "The puppies were awfully hungry, and CERT just did that wild dog round up."

Dan looked at the squirming, furry pups and the joy they were bringing to Will and Erin. "Some wrongs have to be set right, don't they son?" said Dan. "Let's make a plan of action."

The End